Joanne was having trouble breathing

With one hand on the small of her back, Mike pulled her against him. A delicious shudder shook her as she felt his body press against her. Her knees were shaky.

She needed to sit down. Or better yet, lie down. And not on the brickwork of her porch. She murmured in Mike's ear, "Why don't we go inside?"

Mike stiffened. His hands dropped away from her. "I don't think we'd better do that, Joanne."

Joanne flushed with embarrassment. "I see, well . . ." she muttered inanely.

"It's just that if I came in, I'm certain we'd make love," he explained.

Exactly what she'd had in mind. She could feel her flush deepening. At least, she kept herself from saying anything dumb. Instead, she said nothing.

Mike seemed to tower over her, virile, aroused. But his voice was gentle. "And I never go to bed with a woman on the first date."

When **Karen Percy** was writing *Love Counts*, she liked her heroine's well-to-do, slightly kooky best friend so much that Karen felt her character deserved a story of her own. She decided to explore what would happen if Joanne Stephenson met a man from an entirely different world. Enter swimming-pool contractor Mike Balthazar—practical, down-to-earth and absolutely convinced, in the famous words of F. Scott Fitzgerald, that "the rich are different from you and me."

Books by Karen Percy

HARLEQUIN TEMPTATION
260—THE HOME STRETCH
346—LOVE COUNTS

Don't miss any of our special offers. Write to us at the following address for information on our newest releases.

Harlequin Reader Service
P.O. Box 1397, Buffalo, NY 14240
Canadian address: P.O. Box 603,
Fort Erie, Ont. L2A 5X3

In Too Deep

KAREN PERCY

Harlequin Books

TORONTO • NEW YORK • LONDON
AMSTERDAM • PARIS • SYDNEY • HAMBURG
STOCKHOLM • ATHENS • TOKYO • MILAN

Published September 1991

ISBN 0-373-25464-4

IN TOO DEEP

1

JOANNE STEPHENSON lay on the redwood deck behind her new house, sweating. Beads of perspiration stood out all over her body, except on the relatively insignificant percentage of her anatomy that was covered by her fluorescent yellow bikini.

Not far from her head, Joanne had placed a cassette player. Out of its tiny speaker, a female voice slowly enunciated, *"Ja potrebujem zatku do mojej vane."*

"Ja...potre—bujem..." Joanne repeated. She halted when she completed translating the sentence from Czech to English—"I need a stopper for my bathtub drain." *What a stupid thing to learn!* If, on her long-anticipated trip to Prague in a few months, she ended up in a hotel room with a tub lacking a stopper, she'd stuff a washcloth in the drain hole.

She rolled over and pressed the Stop button. Having roasted her back and front the maximum ten minutes—all the sun time her fair, freckled skin could take—she stood up.

Joanne loved soaking up the sun. What she loved even *more* was leaping into a pool to cool off. Vigorous laps, of course, had the added benefit of keeping her body in decent shape. At forty plus—and only her *very* best friends knew what that "plus" represented in actual years—those laps were essential.

The problem was her new house had no pool. Why had she bought a house without a pool? Why had she bought a new house at all, for that matter, when there had been nothing wrong with the old one?

The theory behind it had been reasonable. The younger of her two sons was entering college in the fall. The old house was too big for just her. So she would do the sensible thing—she had announced to her friends—and move to a smaller place. Her friends—who had politely *not* expressed their surprise that Joanne would do something governed purely by common sense—had agreed that it was a good idea.

A very good idea. The only trouble was that she had fallen in love with *this* house. It was in a canyon in a suburb of Los Angeles. In the canyon were oak trees; a tiny stream meandered down the hillside and crossed a corner of her backyard.

The stream and the trees probably would have been enough to entice her—but there was more: The house had spacious rooms, cool tile floors, and a beehive fireplace in the master bedroom.

In love with the house, Joanne allowed nothing to stand in her way—not even the fact that it was five hundred square feet larger than her old one. When some of her friends chuckled and said, "Isn't that just like Joanne?" she disregarded their comments and went ahead and made an offer.

Before she knew it, the old house was sold and the new house officially hers. The one thing she hadn't considered was timing. She'd moved in a week before. Now here she was, a week into July, and it was turning out to be one of the hottest Julys on record in Southern California. Naturally there was air conditioning indoors, but no pool.

Not yet.

She went to the edge of the redwood deck. She picked up the end of a coiled green garden hose and gave the faucet handle a full turn. Holding the hose over her head, she doused herself thoroughly, until her wildly curling red hair hung in straight wet strings down her neck and the sweat on her body was rinsed away by the cool water.

She turned off the hose, then picked up the oversize beach towel she had lain on and draped it around her neck. One of the great things about having tile floors inside the house was that she didn't have to worry about dripping on carpets.

As she slid open the glass door leading to the house, she heard the front doorbell chime. She was expecting several people this afternoon: a plumber to repair one of the upstairs toilets, which gurgled for at least two minutes after it flushed; a person from the gas company to check out the heater, and best of all, a man who built swimming pools. But none of them was scheduled to arrive this early.

Not that she was complaining. The sooner she got things straightened out, the sooner she could get back into her normal, hectic schedule.

Her bare feet slapped on the red tile floors as she hurried through the enormous room that stretched from the back to the front of the house. The room's function changed—it started off as a breakfast area at the back then became a casual den in the center, and ended up as a formal living room.

The outer areas were straightened out, but the center section was stacked with cardboard boxes that were filled with...stuff. Junk like two cartons full of golf trophies that belonged to Doug, her ex-husband of nearly six years.

Making a mental note to call him and see what he wanted her to do with his "treasures," she went on to the foyer. Assuming it had to be one of the people she was expecting, she opened the front door.

On her doorstep stood a very large man. It wasn't even that he was so tall—just about six feet—but he was brawny. He had wide shoulders, a well-developed chest and powerful biceps.

His face was rugged looking with a strong prominent nose and jutting jaw. His dark brown hair, threaded with gray, was thick and wiry.

Eyes that were very blue focused on her dripping, bikini-clad body.

No uniform, so he wasn't from the gas company. That meant he was either the plumber or the pool builder. Before she could ask which he was, he said brusquely, "Wrong house. Sorry I bothered you."

"You didn't..." Joanne began, but he had already turned and started down the steps leading to the street.

"...bother me," she finished to the air. Too bad he wasn't the plumber, she reflected, watching his firm muscular behind as he strode away from her. He looked highly competent—the kind of man who could fix not only a gurgling toilet, but just about anything he put his mind to.

At the curb, he disappeared from view. The phone rang as she shut the door. She sighed. Her answering machine was still missing—in one of the unpacked boxes...but which one?

She hurried back to the breakfast area. From there, she could gaze through the floor-to-ceiling windows at the greenery on the rising slope of her backyard. Eventually, she would be able to look out at her pool. She could hardly wait.

She picked up the phone.

"Mrs. Stephenson?" inquired a voice whose nasal, penetrating quality Joanne had come to detest. "This is Marilyn Burnham at the Elite Employment Agency."

"Yes, Ms. Burnham?" she said.

"I understand you've decided not to employ Mrs. Rodriguez as your housekeeper."

Wilma Thompson, Joanne's longtime housekeeper and mainstay, had decided to retire and spend more time with her grandchildren. For the past three days, Joanne had been interviewing potential replacements.

"That's right," she said.

"But why? Mrs. Rodriguez is a *treasure*. Her previous employers have given her the *highest* recommendations."

Joanne tightened her grasp on the telephone. It was time to take a tough line with Ms. Burnham, make her understand that there were certain requirements in an employee that she wasn't going to waive, no matter what.

"She may be a treasure, Ms. Burnham. I have no doubt that she's a wonderful housekeeper and cook. Her references were certainly glowing enough. But she is also a bore, Ms. Burnham. A bore and a stick and a . . . a *prune*."

"A prune?" Ms. Burnham echoed in astonished tones.

"Yes, a prune," Joanne stated decisively. "Do you know, she didn't smile once the whole time we were talking?"

MIKE BALTHAZAR sat in the driver's seat of his van, holding the cellular phone to his ear. He'd debated long and hard over whether his car phone's value to his business made it worth the expense. He was well aware that his background of poverty made him inclined to examine and reexamine every dollar. However, the car phone had indeed proved its worth, especially in situations like today's.

He dialed the office number and his daughter-in-law, Kitty, who worked for him as a receptionist-secretary, answered, "Balthazar Pools."

"Hi, it's Dad." As always when he talked to Kitty, he forced more warmth into his tone than he actually felt. He didn't *dis*like her, exactly. He just wished she weren't quite so bossy with his son, Bill. Bill didn't seem to mind though. Besides it was their business after all, not his, as Mike frequently reminded himself.

"I seem to have the wrong address for the two o'clock estimate," he told Kitty.

"Two o'clock? But, Dad, it's not even one yet."

"I know. I'm running ahead of schedule."

"Oh, okay. Let me check the log." There was a pause and then she reported, "Two o'clock is Ms. Stephenson . . . Joanne Stephenson, 8417 Hillwood Drive."

Mike glanced at the topmost slip of paper on the clipboard lying on the seat beside him. The street name and numbers matched. What had thrown him off was that woman. The sight of her in a bathing suit and dripping wet seemed to him strong evidence indicating the existence of a pool. Therefore, she couldn't be the woman who wanted an estimate for a brand-new one.

Normally he wouldn't have left so abruptly. He would have asked if he had the right house, inquiring if there were Stephensons in the neighborhood. But the sight of her, nearly naked and with beads of water clinging to her skin, had had a powerful and potentially embarrassing effect on him. There was still a residual tightness in his groin. He couldn't think when he'd been so affected by the sight of a woman's body.

Funny thing, he thought, a slight grin curving his mouth. Just last week he'd been having a beer with his old friend Al. Unlike Mike, who had been a widower for nearly four years now, Al was recently divorced. And frustrated.

"What happened to the women with breasts?" Al had complained. "And hips. They used to have hips, didn't they? When you grabbed them back in the old days, at least you got a good feel of something before they slapped you."

Mike had agreed. It seemed to him that too many women nowadays dieted themselves to the point of looking anorexic. But he could now inform Al that at least one female with breasts and hips still lived. In a house on Hillwood Drive. A ritzy neighborhood—so the woman with the superlative physical endowments must be some rich guy's wife.

Or was she?

Ms. Stephenson, Kitty had said. And that *could* mean she didn't have a husband. He hadn't noticed a ring, but then, considering the spectacular view on display, he hadn't been noticing her hands.

Not that it mattered. Husband or no, she was way out of *his* league. The neighborhood she lived in was proof enough of that.

"By the way, Kitty, when you set up the appointment for Ms. Stephenson, did she happen to mention a husband?"

"No, I'm sure she didn't." Kitty's voice sharpened with curiosity. "Why do you want to know?"

"No reason," he said hastily. "I just wondered if I'd have to do a sales pitch to him, too, or just to her."

"Sales pitch!" She laughed. "I know your idea of a pitch, Dad."

Mike tried not to sound defensive. "We do okay without using high-pressure tactics." He figured quality workmanship and the best materials ought to speak for themselves, and usually they did. Balthazar Pools was highly regarded in the construction industry.

"That's true," Kitty agreed. "As a matter of fact, it seems to me you've been awfully busy lately, Dad. Couldn't Bill—"

This wasn't the time for a discussion of his schedule. Not at the rates they charged for a call on a cellular phone. He cut her off. "Sorry, Kitty. I've got to go."

He *had* been busy lately—doing estimates, talking with potential clients as well as actual ones, checking each phase of the jobs that were currently under way. That was nothing to complain about. His attitude, as he summed it up to his son, was simple: Work hard and keep working, because *you just never know.*

As he got back out of his van, Mike felt a sense of anticipation—strictly for business reasons, he told himself. In a neighborhood like this, for a house like the one Ms. Stephenson owned, it was bound to be a big job; nothing but the best. That meant a higher profit margin for Balthazar Pools, and one more layer of cushioning against potential disaster. *You just never know.*

He permitted himself a wry smile. Then again, there *was* the off chance that Ms. Stephenson might still be wearing that bikini.

HAVING FINISHED TELLING Marilyn Burnham what was what, Joanne was on her way to the stairs, intending to go up to her bedroom and get dressed, when the doorbell rang again.

In the foyer, she stood on tiptoe to peer through the peephole. Fascinating. It was *him* again—the specimen with the muscles.

Suddenly she realized how little of her was covered by her bikini. She took the oversize towel she'd been carrying around with her ever since she left the backyard and wrapped it around herself, sarong-style, before opening the door.

"Right house, after all," he said succinctly. "I'm Mike Balthazar. Balthazar Pools."

"The pool man!" she cried rapturously, then realized she had inadvertently used the phrase that normally described the people who came around each week to pour chlorine and skim leaves. And Mike Balthazar was not a "pool man," but a swimming-pool contractor. Not only did he come highly recommended for the quality of his work, the pools he'd built had won numerous awards.

"That's right," he told her. "I'm running a little ahead of schedule today. I hope you don't mind me showing up early."

"I don't mind a bit." She narrowed her eyes at him. "One question, though. Why did you go away before?"

"When I see a wet woman in a bathing suit, I generally figure she got that way swimming—" he paused "—in a *pool*. In that case, you'd have had no need for me to build one for you. Wearing your swimsuit in the shower, were you?"

"Under the garden hose."

"Oh, of course. I should have figured that."

He had a nice rumbly voice, Joanne decided.

She smiled. "Not necessarily. I'd say it was a perfectly natural mistake." She stepped back to give him room to enter. "Please come in, Mr. Balthazar."

He stepped inside and closed the door behind him.

She extended her hand. "I'm Joanne Stephenson. I know you've figured that out, but we might as well make it official."

It was a deliberate ploy on Joanne's part. She had a firm, if admittedly not entirely rational belief, that a handshake revealed inner truths about a person. She even had proof that it worked. There was that stockbroker she'd gone out with once or twice. *His* handshake had been so moist and squirmy that she hadn't been the least bit surprised when the news media reported his involvement in a stock fraud.

Mike Balthazar's hand came out to meet hers. With the first touch of skin to skin, Joanne knew it would be all right—he wouldn't abscond for parts unknown with her deposit or try to bully her into having some feature she didn't want in her pool, just to add to the price. This was the handshake of an honest man. Dry, firm and strong—without being overbearing.

And then, just when she was feeling comfortable because Mike Balthazar had passed her test, the handshake became something else. A current seemed to flow between them, and heat rose up Joanne's arm, spreading throughout her body.

She couldn't think how long it had been since she'd felt anything that strong: pure, primitive male-female stuff on a stunningly intense level.

When their hands separated, Joanne frowned. She had no idea if Mike Balthazar had had the same kind of reaction as she.

Funny. Her radar must be temporarily out of whack. She was usually fairly adept at picking up on things like that. Boy, she was glad she'd wrapped the towel around herself, because she was certain that the zing she'd gotten from that handshake had been enough to make her nipples stiffen. She wouldn't ordinarily have been embarrassed by her body's natural responses—but from a *handshake?* That was ridiculous!

Resisting the impulse to cross her arms in front of her, she said, "Look, I don't know what the procedure is on this pool thing. And I really would like to put some clothes on before we talk."

He looked as if he'd have liked to say something at that point, but he didn't.

She went on, "In the meantime, why don't you take a look at the backyard?" She smiled. "I thought that was where I'd put the pool."

"What a good idea! I never would have thought of that!" he said dryly.

Her smile widened. Another plus for Mike Balthazar. A sense of humor.

"And you call yourself a pool contractor!" she teased. "Follow me."

As she led him out of the living area into the next section of the room, she quipped, "Watch your step. This is where I keep my priceless collection of antique cardboard boxes."

He guffawed—an honest-sounding guffaw from deep in his chest. Joanne chuckled along with him as she detoured around a box. If this man wasn't taken—which he almost certainly was—she could *easily* fall in love with him.

MIKE BALTHAZAR was standing in the backyard by himself. He was glad of it, considering that Ms. Stephenson—even with a giant towel concealing her enticing bare skin—*still* had a powerful effect on him.

It was pure lust. That was all it could be. And for a potential client. Wasn't *that* businesslike! he told himself sarcastically.

He turned his attention to the yard. All he could do now was take a preliminary survey. Without soil cores and geological checks, he wouldn't be able to determine much. Instead of viewing the site, he should have asked to see the plans her landscape architect had drawn up.

He took in the slope of the hill, the little stream at the edge of the lot, the wild-looking vegetation. He hoped Ms. Stephenson's architect had taken advantage of the natural landscape. If it were up to him, he'd try to make it look like a woodland pool—the kind of place where you might glance up to find a doe and her fawn lapping at the water. Tricky, but it could be done....

JOANNE DREW a deep breath as she slid open the glass door. Mike Balthazar had his back to her, seemingly lost in contemplation of her yard.

Upstairs in her room, the desire to look as good as possible for an attractive man had warred with her fear that to dally too long would be inconsiderate. Her compromise had been to slip on a full-skirted sundress, jam her feet into backless sandals and confine her makeup to a touch of lipstick and mascara. By accomplishing all this at ninety miles an hour, she still had a few moments to do something about her wet hair.

Attacking it with the blow drier turned on high and a vigorously wielded brush had made it a slightly damp semblance of its usual tumble of curls.

Anxious about Mike Balthazar's reaction to her rejuvenated appearance, she inhaled and started across the redwood deck.

Hearing footsteps, Mike turned and took a good *long* look at the woman walking toward him. There couldn't be a more pleasing sight than the way Joanne Stephenson had looked the *first* time he'd seen her. Her present incarnation, however, was every bit as good. Because of that hair. Dry, it flamed around her face, catching sparks of sunlight.

Smiling, she came up to him. "How does it look?"

"Terrific," he blurted, then realized she must be referring to her yard. Quickly he added, "An interesting challenge. But I'll have to see your architect's plans before I can get even a rough idea of what we're talking about here."

"Oh, of course. I should have realized. Come on back inside, and I'll show you."

Moments later, Mike was seated at the glass-topped table. Obviously, this was the heart of the house for Ms. Stephenson, the way the kitchen was in his own modest home less than ten miles from hers. A newspaper, open and folded at the crossword puzzle, rested on the table. Next to it was an open engagement book and a pad of paper whose topmost sheet was filled with a To Do list.

Joanne handed him the rolled-up plans. "Can I get you something to drink?" she offered politely.

"A glass of water would be nice," he replied and unrolled the plans.

When she returned from the kitchen, she set a glass down on the table.

"Thanks," he murmured without looking up from the large sheets he held out in front of him.

Joanne pulled out the wicker chair beside his and sat down. She watched him studying the design she'd paid a hefty fee for. The landscape architects she'd hired had come highly recommended. Not blessed with an artist's eye, she had to assume that their design was a good one. Still . . . there was something not quite right about the plans and sketches.

Mike looked as if he agreed. His mouth was slightly downturned, and between his strongly etched brows were two vertical lines.

"Something wrong?" Joanne asked after a while.

His expression was troubled. "Oh, no . . . Hanson and Barnes—" he named the architects responsible. "—is a fine firm. I've worked with them before."

"But you don't like what they came up with," Joanne surmised.

Mike looked down at the plans. They were fine for a manicured, suburban backyard, he supposed, but all wrong for this site.

He forced a smile. "It doesn't really matter if I like it or not, does it? It's your pool, Ms. Stephenson."

"Call me Joanne," she said. "But I'm not sure I like the design either. I don't know why."

He hesitated. "I think I can tell you why. What this site needs is something natural, maybe tying the stream in with it and . . ."

He went on speaking, sketching curves in the air with his hand. What he described seemed like utter heaven to Joanne. She nodded enthusiastically. "That's it! That's what I want! When can you start?"

Mike rocked back in her chair. "Start? But, Ms. Stephenson—"

"Joanne," she reminded him.

"Joanne . . . you'd need to have sketches made, plans drawn up, to see exactly what you want."

"Fine. You draw them."

"I'm not a landscape architect."

"You don't have to be, do you? No, I know you don't. I checked that out before I started this project. There's no law that says you have to have a degree to design and build a pool. Contractors do it all the time. You've done it before, haven't you? I mean, when a customer didn't want to bother with an architect?"

"Well, yes," Mike admitted reluctantly. But he'd never worked on a project this complex without an architect. Judging from Hanson and Barnes's plans, she wanted the best in materials and technology.

She leaned forward and put her hand on his forearm. "Please," she said. Her touch, along with the low, seductive tone of her voice, made Mike's muscles tense.

Joanne felt his response and her heart thumped. She'd wanted her pool put in as quickly as possible. Now she wasn't sure she was in all that much of a hurry, after all. She imagined many meetings with this man. Many *long* meetings. . . .

Only there was still the possibility of him being married. Could she just come right out and ask him?

At that moment, the phone rang. Joanne reluctantly took her hand from Mike's arm. Before she dealt with this untimely interruption, she'd try to get a promise from him to design the pool he'd described.

"You will do it, won't you, Mike?" she asked earnestly.

"I guess I could make some sketches," he told her with obvious reluctance. "You can see if you like them after we've gone that far. Uh . . . your phone is ringing."

Joanne picked it up. "Chang's Chinese Laundry," she answered, hoping to discourage the party on the other end if it was an insurance salesman or an aluminum-siding man. A friend would recognize her voice.

A friend did. A waspish tenor said, "You know, I usually love your sense of humor, darling, but not today."

"Oh, hi, Warren." Warren Frostine, financial pundit, not only managed her money, but was her regular escort—whenever she wasn't dating someone more interesting.

"Please, no cheer, either. I'm dying. It's that awful flu that's going around."

"I'm sorry. Should I play sister of mercy and bring you some chicken soup?"

"Spare me. You don't have a housekeeper yet, do you? I know your cooking. It's obviously escaped what you like to call your mind, angel, that you and I had a date to do our Fred-and-Ginger imitation tonight. Not to mention Alison Colfax's dreary dinner before the ball."

Joanne *had* forgotten. Completely. Tonight was an important event for one of the charities she supported—an organization that supplied food and clothing for the homeless. As a member of the planning committee, she absolutely had to go. And she couldn't go alone. "You can't do this to me, Warren. I have to have a date. What am I going to do?"

"I don't know, sweet puss. I can tell you what *I'm* going to do, however. Retire to my teeny-tiny cot and moan."

"Take care of yourself, Warren," Joanne said distractedly. She'd just had an idea. Casting a covert glance at the man seated across from her, she thought, *Why not?* The worst that could happen would be that he'd turn out to be married or attached or busy—or he would turn her down for some other reason. She might end up feeling a little foolish for having invited him, but one of the things she'd learned over the years was that no one died from feeling like a fool.

She hung up the phone and faced Mike.

"Something wrong?" he asked.

"You might say so." She leaned forward and propped her chin in her hand. "Let's play a little game. I'm going to ask you three questions, requiring only yes-or-no answers. Give the correct answers and you win a prize."

He smiled good-humoredly. "What's the prize? Shouldn't you tell me that first?"

"It's a mystery prize," she said blandly. "Ready for the questions?"

"I guess."

She lifted her chin out of her hand and held up her first finger. "One: Are you married? Two: Or otherwise committed? And three: If the answers to one and two are 'No,' will you go out with me tonight?"

2

JOANNE SMILED to herself as she dialed her best friend, Lindsay Reynolds. With six-month-old twins and a thriving accountancy partnership, Lindsay and her husband, Tim, had a *very* hectic life. Even so, Joanne knew Lindsay would want to hear *right away* about this interesting new development in her life. After all, she and Lindsay had been confiding in each other since high school.

While giving her name to Tim and Lindsay's receptionist, she felt just the way she had in high school. Her insides were jumpy. A smile kept popping onto her face for no reason—as if she were sixteen again and had a date with the cutest boy in class.

The receptionist finally put her through. "Guess what!" Joanne burst out. "I've got a date tonight for that charity thing. A *real* date! Not Warren."

"That's terrific!" Lindsay exclaimed. "Who is he? Where'd you meet him? Tell me all!"

Joanne told her the whole story—in minute detail. Then she gleefully added, "He's not married and he's not involved. That's what he said. I'm *sure* he was telling the truth." She grinned, remembering the expression on Mike's face. "He looked much too startled to be lying."

"And he agreed to go to dinner and the dance—just like that?"

"Well, I didn't exactly mention the dance part of the evening," Joanne admitted. "You know how some men are about dancing. Mention the word and they develop a burning need to watch the basketball game or something. I said it was a dinner, followed by a charity do and I really needed an escort." She giggled. "I did it properly, too. Offered to pick him up on his doorstep and everything. I even thought about buying him a corsage, but I decided that might be going too far."

"I'll say." Lindsay laughed. "So you're picking him up?"

"Well, no, actually I'm not. He got a little stuffy about that. He said being asked out by a woman was okay, but when it came to a member of the opposite sex chauffeuring him around, he was putting his foot down. 'Take it or leave it,' he said."

"And you took it," Lindsay guessed.

"You bet," Joanne confirmed cheerfully. "Listen, Linds, guys like this don't grow on trees. At least not in any orchards I've visited lately."

LATE THAT AFTERNOON, Mike pulled his van into a parking space in front of the flat, one-story stucco office building that housed Balthazar Pools.

As he walked toward the door, wondering if his gray suit—the one he hardly ever wore—was in a fit state for tonight, he noticed that the company's pickup truck was parked a few spaces away. Bill must be done for the day, too.

Hearing Kitty shouting, he paused outside the office door. "No *way!* I can't stand Johnny Jacoby and you know it! And you're not going to go running around with him without me. You can just forget it. Tell him you're busy."

Mike winced. He hated to hear Kitty and Bill argue. This time, though, he agreed with Kitty that the Jacoby boy was a loser. Twenty-three—the same age as Bill—and he still hadn't settled into a job. But Bill and Johnny had been good friends since they were in elementary school.

Through the still-closed door, he couldn't hear Bill's soft reply. Mike had no doubt but that his son was giving in to his wife—again.

He turned the knob and deliberately bumped the door as he pushed it open. Evidently the noise was sufficient warning because Kitty looked up, smiling brightly, as if she hadn't been ranting at her husband a moment before.

Bill stood near his wife's desk, his shoulders slightly slumped. He had his mother's brown eyes and full mouth. His body was a less well-developed version of his father's.

Pretending he hadn't heard a thing, Mike said cheerfully, "Hey, kids!"

"Hi, Dad. How you doing?" Bill said.

"Fine." Mike set his briefcase down just inside the door. "How's the Granger job going?" Mike had meant to get by the Granger place himself today, to double-check that everything was proceeding smoothly, but he hadn't managed to.

"Fine. Ready to start the tiling."

Mike nodded. "Have you scheduled Hector yet?" In Mike's opinion, Hector Andrade was the best tile man in the business.

"I called him, but he's busy until next week. I thought maybe I'd get Jim Dougherty instead."

Mike shook his head. "Wait for Hector."

"But the Grangers are getting impatient."

"They'll be worse than impatient if the tiling isn't done right," Mike told him, trying to keep the irritation out of his voice. "Wait for Hector."

Bill nodded reluctantly. Mike then asked Kitty, "Anything here I need to know about?" He hated falling behind. He was always juggling several jobs and on the lookout for new work. It was easier since Bill had joined him in the business. Still, it would be a while yet before Bill would be ready to take full responsibility for a job—from the first contact with the client right through to completion.

Kitty pointed to a stack of pink memo slips skewered on a wood-based holder. "You had quite a few calls, but nothing urgent."

He noticed that she was wearing her dishwater-blond hair pulled up in a ponytail. She looked better with it down. Loose, it made her narrow face and pointed nose look less sharp.

The thought of hair brought to mind Joanne's red curls. He envisioned those curls brushing his bare chest and—

He cut off that line of thought.

Why on earth had he ever agreed to go out with Joanne Stephenson? Right from the start, he'd made up his mind that giving in to his attraction to her would be a mistake. Not only was she a potential client, but her impulsiveness and kookiness both intrigued and dismayed him. And then there was her obvious wealth. He was sure they would have nothing in common—absolutely *no* basis for a relationship.

But he'd been so surprised when she asked him out that he'd said yes.

Why make such a big deal over one date? She'd needed an escort and he was handy. That was all there was to it. What harm could one evening do? And it might even provide an amusing glimpse at how the other half lived.

He glanced at the clock on the wall behind the desk. "I've got to get going."

"Going?" Bill sounded puzzled. "I thought the three of us were going to grab a bite to eat and go bowling this evening. We need the practice before the tournament starts." All three of them were members of a local bowling league. The big tournament for the year was scheduled for August.

Bill had mentioned something about that the day before, Mike vaguely recalled, but the plans hadn't seemed definite. "Sorry, I won't be able to tonight, after all."

It was Kitty who pressed him. "Why not?"

"Other plans," Mike said evasively.

"Why, Dad," Kitty responded, sounding surprised, "have you got a date?"

"Uh, something like that." He made a big production out of glancing at his watch, even though he'd looked at the wall clock less than thirty seconds before. "Gotta dash," he announced. Then, before either Kitty or Bill could ask him any more questions—like *who* his date was with, for instance—he turned and left the office.

AT SEVEN O'CLOCK, Joanne's doorbell rang. She hurried down the stairs, thankful that the slit in the skirt of her black dress permitted some freedom of movement. Actually, the dress was quite conservative, with long sleeves and a not-too-terribly low neckline. Her billowing hair added color to her all-black ensemble.

She could just imagine how hunky Mike would look in a black tux—with those shoulders of his filling it out.

What a vision the two of them would make on the dance floor—assuming, that is, that she could get him onto the dance floor.

As she opened the door to him, she felt a twinge of dismay. He wasn't wearing a tux. Hadn't she told him that everyone would be in evening dress? Come to think of it, no, she hadn't. She had assumed he'd know.

But why *should* he have known? There weren't many people nowadays who attended dances and parties in formal dress. Life in Southern California was loose and casual.

For that matter, this kind of evening wasn't her style, either—except it was for a worthy cause. Since her sons had grown up, the many charities she did volunteer work for had become practically a full-time job.

"Hi, come in. I'll be ready in a sec." To hide her concern, she injected a note of gaiety into her voice. Dressed as he was, Mike was more than likely to feel out of place this evening.

Mike gave her an acute glance. "Something wrong?"

So much for her ability to conceal her emotions! "No, not a thing!" she lied. "I'll be ready to go in a sec. All I have to do is get my wrap and turn my answering machine on. *Finally* I found it. It was in a box with my sons' old report cards and school stuff. Can you believe it? I can't imagine how on earth it got in *there*."

She turned away from Mike. Before she could take a step, his hand curved over the top of her shoulder. "Wait a minute."

She turned her head back to look at him, and the tip of her chin brushed his knuckles. Though accidental, it felt remarkably like a caress. A shiver raced down her spine.

Mike's fingers tightened for an instant before he released her. "I'm dressed wrong," he stated flatly.

She couldn't deny it. "You look wonderful," she countered.

"Thanks. So do you. However..."

One wrong word, Joanne thought, and he was going to turn around and march right out of here. Quickly, she pivoted so she stood beside him, then slipped her arm into his and rested her hand on his forearm. "I'm sorry," she said in confidential tones. "I'm an idiot. I should have warned you that people were going to be in fancy getups."

"Yes, you should. If you had, I might have been able to rent a tux. I don't own one," he added.

"No reason why you should." She paused. "Look, Mike, if you feel uncomfortable about it, let's just not go. I'll change into something—" she gestured down at herself with her free hand "—less ridiculous, and we'll...I don't know...go have dinner somewhere quiet."

And she'd just have to make up some excuse for her committee members as to why she failed to appear. A mild case of bubonic plague, perhaps. She'd also have to call Alison Colfax, who was expecting Joanne and her escort for dinner less than half an hour from now. Alison would rant and rave about two empty places at her table, but Joanne could put up with her ranting. Better that than ruining whatever possibilities might exist between her and Mike Balthazar.

Mike shook his head. "It's nice of you to suggest changing your plans. But I distinctly remember you saying it was important for you to go to this thing to-night."

"Well, yes, but—"

"Let me finish! The way I see it, you've got two choices. You can go without me or you can go with me. They won't actually keep us out if I'm not in a tux, will they?"

"No, of course not."

"It's up to you, then. You can choose between being embarrassed by showing up with a guy who's dressed in a suit, or showing up with no guy at all. It's no sweat for me, either way."

He finished with a shrug of his massive shoulders that lifted the smooth fabric of his suit.

A *very* nice suit, Joanne told herself. Much nicer than some of the ratty old tuxes that some of the men would appear in this evening.

She smiled up at Mike. "Embarrassed? Me? When you get to know me a little better, you'll find out that nothing embarrasses Joanne Stephenson." She paused again. "Well, I *might* be embarrassed if you decided to strip off that *very* handsome suit of yours and dance naked on Alison Colfax's dining room table." Although it might be worth it, to get a look at Mike Balthazar's *very* impressive body.

He grinned. "I can promise you I won't do that."

"Well, let's go then," said Joanne.

"JOANNE, DARLING," Alison Colfax purred, passing her lips through the air a quarter of an inch from Joanne's cheek. Alison was unwisely clad in brilliant emerald-green satin, which cast green highlights onto her sallow complexion.

Beside her, her husband Harvey, looking closer to seventy than the fifty he was, mumbled a greeting. The rather unkind joke in their circle was that Alison had worn Harvey out—not with her sexual demands but with her financial ones.

"And who is this?" Alison asked, stepping back to eye Mike with a look that Joanne compared to the one she'd seen on the face of the buzzard at the zoo one day at feeding time.

Before she could comment about Mike's attire—and Joanne wouldn't have put it past Alison *to* comment— Joanne introduced Mike, then hesitated. She'd been about to add, "Mike is in swimming pools," but she couldn't say *that*. It sounded ridiculous. "I dragooned Mike into this," she substituted. "Wasn't it kind of him to agree to come at the last minute?"

"Oh, very kind," Alison agreed mechanically. To Joanne's relief, she turned to greet the next guests.

Joanne tucked her hand into Mike's arm and steered him into the room. The living room was furnished with what Alison claimed were all genuine French antiques. Joanne suspected that a large number of them were reproductions.

"Quick, let's get a drink," she whispered. "And be warned, they're mostly water. If you want to fortify yourself before dinner, you'll have to down quite a few of them."

Mike gave her a quizzical look. "Why would I want to fortify myself?"

Joanne chuckled. "Because it's bound to be excruciatingly boring, that's why."

Mike looked down at her, puzzled. "If you find these people so boring, then why do you spend time with them?"

Joanne considered how best to explain, and then realized that she *couldn't* explain. Not yet. To tell him about the obligations that came with the wealth she'd inherited would be to announce the extent of that wealth. And her experience had been that she was wisest not to discuss that until she knew a person extremely well.

She sighed. "It's a long story. And besides, not everybody here is boring. Not by a long shot. It's just that somehow, at the dinner table, Alison manages to make it seem that way. She proposes topics of conversation and everybody has to fall in line or she turns that *gaze* on you."

"I saw that gaze," Mike replied with a faint smile.

A waiter passed nearby, carrying a tray of drinks toward a group of people who stood near the spindly-legged love seat that no one ever dared sit on. The waiter got stalled a few feet away, his polite Excuse-me's unheard by the portly gentleman who was blocking his path.

Mike directed a conspiratorial glance at Joanne. "Shall I?" he asked, with a subtle jerk of his head at the waiter's tray.

"By all means," Joanne encouraged with a chuckle.

"Ours, I think," Mike said, and plucked two glasses from the tray.

"But, sir," the waiter protested briefly, then resignedly returned to the bar set up in the hallway.

"That's what I like—a man of action," Joanne said warmly.

"Don't be too pleased until we see what we've got," Mike warned her. He peered down at the glasses. "This looks like Scotch and water. The other one . . ." The second glass was filled with a clear liquid. "Vodka and something."

"Straight vodka, I'd guess," Joanne said. "My bet is that it was for Milly Perkins—the woman over there in blue. She's a smart cookie. She knows that Alison tells the bartender to use a teaspoon instead of a jigger...but he can't pull that trick with straight anything." She shrugged. "You got them for us. You choose."

"No, indeed. Ladies first."

"Thank you, kind sir," she said, deliberately meeting his blue gaze with her own. "So the age of chivalry isn't dead, after all."

Mike appeared as relaxed and comfortable as anyone could be in a room full of strangers. She reached for the vodka, thinking, *It's going to be all right.*

IT'S GOING ALL WRONG, Joanne thought an hour and a half later as dinner was drawing to a close. Or it had already gone—irretrievably wrong?

She battled down a surge of anger. The people at this gathering weren't *all* snobs, she tried to assure herself. Jonathan Rogers and his wife Kathleen—as well as several of the others—had been perfectly friendly and pleasant to Mike. But she would have given big bucks if George Bentinger hadn't come over to make conversation before dinner.

She eyed Bentinger now. He was seated several places up the table, a middle-aged man with smooth, prematurely white hair and a smug expression. He was Old Money, like Joanne. That seemed to make George think he had a right to approve or disapprove of what Joanne did and the people she saw. Normally, she would just have ignored George. She'd had plenty of practice ig-

noring him, since they'd known each other practically
from birth—but tonight it had been impossible.

He'd dragged his fluffy-brained wife, Anne, over to
where Joanne and Mike were standing with the obvious intention of vetting the stranger in their midst.
George had given Mike an up-and-down perusal that
had sizzled with censure of Mike's "incorrect" attire.
Then he'd begun The Quiz.

The Quiz was designed to discover whether Mike
was suitable or not. The key question concerned Mike's
profession.

In reply, Mike had said politely, "I'm a swimming-
pool contractor."

George hadn't actually sniffed, but he might as well
have. He had dismissed Mike utterly, then regarded
Joanne with an expression that said as clearly as words,
"Where did you find *him?*"

Joanne had promptly vowed never to speak to
George Bentinger again as long as she lived.

But the worst part was that Mike had plainly understood. For George Bentinger and others like him, Mike
Balthazar, swimming-pool contractor—not even wearing the right clothes, for God's sake—simply didn't exist.

Since then, Joanne had watched Mike's tension in-
crease. It was evident in the set of his jaw and the hard,
unrelaxed lines of his shoulders. A couple of the other
men had more or less echoed George's condescending
dismissal. She had put them, too, on her mental list.
And then, only moments before dinner was announced, she'd heard *dear* Alison, her hostess, remark, "Well, all I can say is that he must be *awfully*
good in bed."

She had pretended not to hear and Mike had pretended not to hear. But he *had* heard. And she knew it.

WHAT DIFFERENCE does it make? I'll never see these people again.

Mike had been repeating the same mental phrases over and over like a litany for the past hour. To a certain extent they'd been effective. He hadn't lost his cool. And he was still rational enough to recognize that not *everyone* here had dismissed him as had that Bentinger guy and a couple of his cronies. But the condescension in that—

He cut off the thought, knowing that if he followed through with it, his anger was bound to show in his face. Even though he'd agreed to come, had sworn that nothing that happened this evening would bother him, he could gladly *kill* Ms. Joanne Stephenson for getting him into this.

JOANNE ANXIOUSLY GLANCED down the table to where Mike was sitting next to Bitsy Melrose. No improvement. His brows were lowered, his eyes icy cold. He was furious and she couldn't blame him one bit. The least she could do was get him out of here—now. Even so, she had a piercing fear that he would never forgive her.

Come to think of it, she might never forgive herself.

In a voice deliberately pitched to be loud and clear, she addressed her hostess who was seated at the foot of the table. "Alison, darling, I'm so sorry, but I'm afraid we won't be able to stay for dessert. I need to get to the hotel early to have a few words with the bandleader." It wasn't true, but it would fly as an excuse. One of her jobs, as a member of the planning committee, had been to select and book the band.

"Oh, must you leave so soon?" Alison pealed.

"I'm afraid we must. Mike..."

He looked in her direction, his rugged face bland and blank, although she could still see the daggers in his eyes.

"I'm terribly sorry to tear you away," she said, "but I'm afraid we'll have to go."

Minutes later they were outside, walking the short distance to the sedan Mike drove. The moon was full, shining down on the luxury automobiles driven by the other guests. A light breeze stirred the wispy leaves of the eucalyptus trees lining the street.

All in all, it would have been a romantic stroll to Mike's car—except for the icy fury coming from the man walking beside her. Not closely beside her, but several feet away, as if he needed to keep a distance between them.

For once in her life, Joanne was at a loss for words.

They were almost at the car when both of them spoke at once.

"Look, Mike, I'm—"

His voice was louder than her hesitant utterance. "Great friends you've got."

Joanne inhaled deeply. "Some of them are," she said. "But some of them definitely are not. George Bentinger, for instance, is perfectly horrible. But please believe me, Mike. If I'd had any idea what it would be like, I wouldn't have exposed you to that." She stopped and faced him. "I just... I didn't realize. I didn't know."

The frustration he was feeling seemed to boil up and spill out into his face. With an angry twist of his mouth, he replied, "We make ourselves known by the company we keep, Ms. Stephenson. 'Birds of a feather...' You ever hear that one?"

She deserved that, she realized miserably. There wasn't a damn thing she could say in self-defense.

"Nothing else to say?" he inquired, as if he'd read her mind.

She gave a small shake of her head.

And then he grasped her shoulders in his hands. His grip was strong, just a little short of punishing. He pulled her up, simultaneously lowering his head.

His mouth came down hard on hers, in a kiss that at first was purely an expression of his anger. He ground his lips against hers, forcing his tongue between her teeth. But although there wasn't a spark of tenderness or warmth in it, Joanne couldn't keep from responding. Her nipples tingled and a curl of heat flared in her lower body.

She brought her hands up to his chest to push him away, but just as her palms flattened on his lapels, his mouth softened. His lips moved, still hungry but gentler against hers; and his stabbing tongue tasted and teased.

Suddenly Joanne was overwhelmed by the intense attraction she had felt for Mike since the first moment she'd seen him. Desire pulsed heavily between her legs.

She pursued his tongue back between his lips with her own and slid her hands upward on his chest—what was meant to be a push became a caress.

Then he released her and stood looking down at her. Shaken, she looked back at him.

He swallowed convulsively; she saw the movement in his throat. Then he said brusquely, "Let's go."

In silence, he escorted her to the passenger side of his car. Once he was in the driver's seat he pulled out onto the street.

His voice was level, as if the kiss had been a figment of Joanne's imagination. "You'd better give me directions to this place where the party is. What was it—the Sherman Hotel?"

Astonished, she turned her head to stare at him. "You mean you still want to go? Even after . . ."

"I don't want to go, no," he answered flatly. "Frankly, I'd rather be smeared with honey and staked out on an anthill. But there's one thing you'd know about me, if you knew me at all, Ms. Stephenson. I don't run. And I don't quit. And when I say I'll do something, I do it!"

3

JOANNE SURVEYED the elegantly decorated ballroom and nodded approvingly. Everything looked right. The floral centerpieces on the white-clothed tables were exactly what the committee had wanted—lavish displays of Vanda orchids and plumeria flown in this morning from Hawaii. The flower arrangements would be auctioned off before the evening ended—and the proceeds of the bidding would really help the food bank.

She glanced at the sides of the room. Several different bar stations had been set up. Against one wall was a long buffet table that would be heaped with delicacies for the midnight supper.

She then zeroed in on the bandstand at the far end of the room, relieved to see that everything appeared to be in order. The thin-faced young man she'd negotiated with was standing in front of the rows of chairs and music stands, ready to call his musicians into action the moment people started arriving.

Joanne watched the bandleader hurry toward the door that led to the kitchen, where his musicians were hiding out, enjoying their last minutes of freedom.

She took a step toward the bandstand, meaning to tell him that he didn't have to start the music with only her and Mike present. Then she reconsidered. Conversation between herself and her still-smoldering companion seemed like a bad idea at the moment. Perhaps if she could get him to dance with her . . .

She cleared her throat. "I, uh, need to have a word with the band. Come with me?"

"Sure," he said dully. "I don't have a whole lot else to do at the moment."

They arrived at the front just as most of the band members were taking their seats. Knowing that most of the people attending tonight would be from an older, conservative crowd, Joanne had hired a dance band that specialized in playing music from the thirties and forties.

Asking them to play a slow number right now might not be a bad idea, she decided.

As the thin-faced blond bandleader took his place in front of his musicians, Joanne left Mike standing on the dance floor a few feet away.

"Hi, Ms. Stephenson," the bandleader greeted. "You want us to start?"

"I know there aren't many people here yet," Joanne began. That was an understatement. Not counting the bartenders waiting at their stations, there were precisely two. "But I think it's a good idea to have the music going as people arrive. Is that okay with you?"

"You're the boss."

"In that case, how about something slow—" she lowered her voice "—and sexy."

"'Smoke Gets In Your Eyes'?" he suggested.

"Perfect," Joanne purred.

She turned back toward Mike. There was only one possible flaw in her plan. What if he didn't dance? Or didn't want to dance? Or didn't want to dance with *her*? She couldn't tell how much fury was left in him—and, how much had been leeched away by that kiss.

She walked over to him and stood close as the first strains of the sultry ballad filled the room. "I really hate to ask you another favor, Mike, but would you dance with me? It really helps, you see, if somebody's already dancing as people arrive. It helps get them going . . . start having a good time right away."

"Sure," he replied.

Joanne slid her left hand up onto his shoulder. As he took her right hand, then put his other arm around her waist, she felt a delicious shiver of connection.

They moved in time to the languorous tempo of the music. After a few minutes, Joanne looked up into Mike's face and asked impulsively, "Are you still mad at me?"

He seemed to be lost in a trance. "I'm sorry. What did you say?"

"I asked you if you were still mad at me. Not that you don't have every right to be."

He exhaled a long breath. "I don't much care for some of your friends. But no, I'm not mad at you. Not anymore."

Mike had been mulling over two rather disturbing possibilities. After this evening, he had probably lost any chance of acquiring Ms. Joanne Stephenson as a client. And damn it all, he had wanted to get the chance to design that pool for her.

Yet, to be perfectly honest, deep down he didn't care a hoot about that pool. All he cared about was getting her alone somewhere and making love with her. Tonight. And that was about ten times as disturbing, because he couldn't do that.

To Mike, sex meant having a relationship. And the events of the evening had only reconfirmed his belief that having a relationship with this woman was out of the question. They came from two different worlds.

And he thought *her* world stunk.

"Thank you," Joanne said. "That's really nice of you, Mike."

He couldn't remember what she was talking about, what he was supposed to have done that was so nice. Her perfume seemed to be clouding his brain, making him forget—only temporarily, he reassured himself— that this lady was not for him.

As Joanne let her breasts brush against Mike's chest, she exhaled deeply. She slid her hand up higher on his shoulder so her fingertips brushed the wiry, curling hairs at the back of his neck. She felt the shudder that rippled through him at her light caress and a pulse of heat awoke between her thighs.

They moved slowly, crossing the parquet dance floor inch by inch. Their legs brushed now and then as they moved and contradictory sensations assaulted Joanne's body. She was weightless, light as air, held aloft by the touch of Mike's hands. At the same time she was grow- ing heavier, the increasing heat in her lower body slowing her so she could hardly move.

And now they *were* hardly moving, she realized. Bit by bit, their steps had gotten smaller. It as just as well, because it was too difficult to lift her feet when she felt this way. She felt too heavy, too hot to do much more than sway rhythmically in place.

And yet, there was still space between them. The light contact of the tips of her breasts against Mike's chest had hardened her nipples so that they stung and throbbed. But between his hips and hers was an inch or so that felt like a yawning chasm.

When "Smoke Gets In Your Eyes" ended, the band- leader segued into another slow ballad. Joanne didn't recognize the tune and didn't care. It could have been her all-time favorite and she wouldn't have cared. As the music changed, Mike's hand slid farther down her waist, his fingers splaying down her lower back to pull her hips hard against his.

She let out a muffled gasp of excitement as she felt his full arousal against her belly. He was still keeping up some pretense of moving his feet in rhythm. His hips tilted back and forth in the same tempo, pressing his erection against her, then retreating slightly so that over and over, she experienced the renewed thrill of contact with his hardness.

She had forgotten any pretense of decorum—if she'd had any in the first place. Her breasts were flattened against his chest and the tingling ache in her nipples seemed to force her to move her torso slightly from side to side, rubbing the ache against Mike's chest in hope of obtaining some relief.

But there was no real relief to be had, short of making love, she realized. And there were still hours of the evening to be gotten through before that could happen.

Even so, and even knowing that they'd better back off from each other before she dragged Mike down to the floor and started unbuttoning and unzipping things, she couldn't force herself to pull away from him. It had been so long since she'd felt this way—if she'd *ever* felt quite this much desire before—and it was so *damned* good.

It was both a relief and a devastating disappointment to hear voices filtering through the sensual cloud surrounding her. The band and the bartenders probably hadn't even noticed what she and Mike had been doing with and to each other. Or, if they'd noticed, they certainly wouldn't care. But some of the other party-goers *would* notice. And comment.

She forced herself to pull back against Mike's arm, creating a small gap between them. "I think we'd better stop dancing," she murmured. "People are starting to arrive."

"No!" His tone was sharp, abrupt. His glance down at his lower body was eloquent. "We can't quit dancing yet."

Maybe it was because they were still touching that it took several more tunes, danced with wide inches of space between them, before Mike announced that they could now find their table.

Each white-clothed table seated eight and theirs turned out to be occupied by six other people Joanne didn't know. She was just as glad of that, since the people she *did* know certainly hadn't helped to make it a pleasant evening thus far.

Mike ended up in conversation with one of the men at the table who appeared completely oblivious to Mike's attire.

Joanne chatted with the others at the table while contemplating looking for a complete new set of friends. But she wasn't being fair, she reflected. Her *real* friends—the people she valued, like Lindsay and Tim and Warren—weren't snobs at all. None of them would have acted the way Alison Colfax and George Bentinger had.

It was probably unfortunate that George chose that moment to approach. From the corner of her eye, Joanne saw his white-crowned head nearing their table and focused carefully on the woman across from her. Perhaps, if she pretended not to see George, he would go away.

It didn't work. "Joanne," George said, standing only inches from her.

She didn't look up.

"Joanne," he repeated, more loudly, and he put his hand on her shoulder.

She had to look up at him. As she did so, he reminded, "We haven't had our dance yet. Care to trip the light fantastic?"

Joanne regarded him coldly. "No, thank you."

George jerked his hand from her shoulder as if he'd been burned. Then, with a dismissive glance that encompassed both Mike and Joanne, he strode away.

Mike leaned closer to her and, in a voice pitched for her ears alone, murmured, "You didn't have to do that."

"Yes, I did."

Mike frowned. He couldn't stand that Bentinger guy, but it seemed wrong—all wrong—for him to have created a rift between Joanne and her friends. Just another example of why they shouldn't be together, couldn't be together in the future. They'd barely met, and already he'd disrupted her life.

"THAT'S IT, FOLKS," said the man who had auctioned off the floral displays and supervised the drawing for the prizes donated by various companies. Neither Joanne nor Mike had won anything, but Joanne didn't mind at all. She and Mike had danced seven or eight more times. Seemingly by mutual consent, they had sat out for long stretches because... if they'd gone on dancing, they would have been all over each other right out there on the floor. Even now, when they hadn't touched for at least half an hour, her breasts felt taut and between her thighs she was still damp and hot.

This morning, she mused, she would never even have considered the possibility that tonight she might go to bed with a man she'd only met that afternoon. But now, it seemed beyond possible, and was moving into the realm of the inevitable. Two people who sizzled together the way she and Mike sizzled were *going* to do something about it, PDQ.

PDQ couldn't come any too soon for her, she reflected. Thank God that now the speeches and the auctioning and prize drawing were over, they could leave. She leaned over and touched Mike's hand, which rested on the white-clothed table. He jerked as if he'd been touched by a live wire, and turned toward her.

"I'm ready to go, if you are," she said, "but I need to make a quick trip to the powder room first."

He nodded and she rose. "Back in a minute."

As she entered the ladies' room, Joanne was smiling to herself in anticipation of what was bound to happen when she and Mike got back to her house. Her smile faded abruptly as she saw Alison Colfax seated on a little gold chair in front of the mirror.

Without speaking, she started to walk through to the toilet area, but Alison spotted her in the mirror. "Why, hello, Joanne. Are you having a nice time?"

Joanne considered her reply carefully. Too carefully and for too long, because before she could speak, Alison drawled, "Your friend is...quite attractive. He does seem a bit... *untraveled*, though."

Joanne rounded on her. "Alison, so help me, no one has used that word to mean what you mean since about 1914. I'm embarrassed to admit that I never realized before what a snob you are. And a few other people who were at your party tonight."

Alison's penciled eyebrows rose. "Really, Joanne... So heated about it. I only said—"

"I heard what you said. And I also heard your remark before dinner. In case you're curious, you're absolutely right. Mike is extraordinarily good in bed. A whole hell of a lot better than Harvey, I'd guess. Unless, of course, good old Harv wakes up when he hits the sack, but I wouldn't think that'd be very likely. He's half asleep all the rest of the time." She cocked her head to one side. "Maybe you bore him, Alison."

"Why, why—" Alison sputtered.

"You asked for it," Joanne snapped, then swept on through the swinging door that separated the two areas of the rest room.

When she reemerged, Alison was gone.

MIKE LOOKED UP to see Joanne approaching. Her color was high as she was walking fast. Something must have happened to upset her.

"Anything wrong?" he asked as she jerked her wrap off the back of the chair next to Mike's.

"Not a thing," she answered. "I'm just ready to go, that's all."

She had cooled down—at least in one sense of the phrase—by the time he'd parked his car in front of her house. She was no longer burning with anger. But the other kind of burning, the *good* kind, hadn't lessened in the slightest. Just glancing at Mike's profile as he drove had kept her desire for him alive.

On the way home, they'd even had some pleasant conversation. Joanne had mentioned her sons, explaining that the boys were both away for the summer—Robbie working as a camp counselor and Jeff in France on an exchange program. "They're pretty much gone from home, now," she said. "Jeff, my youngest, is going to college in the fall and that's about it, I guess, except for visits."

"Does it bother you, not having a kid at home anymore?" Mike asked.

"No, not really. Oh, I miss them, of course, but I figure I'm just entering another phase of my life."

She had gone on to ask if he had children. He wasn't especially forthcoming. Still, he had told her a little about Bill and Kitty—both of whom worked in the business with him.

"That's a father's dream, isn't it?" Joanne asked. "To build up something he can pass on to his son?"

"I guess it is. And I guess I'm lucky that Bill seems to want it. I really don't think I'm forcing anything on him."

"I'm sure you're not," Joanne said. "You'd know if he were resisting."

"Yeah, I think I would."

That had brought them to the front of Joanne's house. He walked her to the door. There, key in hand, she turned to him.

"I know you didn't have a very good time," she told him, "and I'm really sorry. But thank you for coming, anyway. I really appreciate it."

After their previous kiss, after how closely they'd been entwined on the dance floor, it didn't even feel particularly bold—just natural and right—for her to rise on tiptoe, offering her mouth for his kiss.

He might have been taken off guard, but he responded. His tongue invaded her mouth, tasting of the single brandy he'd drunk late in the evening. With one hand on the small of her back, he pulled her against him. A delicious shudder shook her as she felt his erection rising and pressing into her.

Then, angling to make some space between them, he placed his palm on her breast. He groaned from deep

in his chest as he tested its weight and fullness. Then he
flicked his thumb over her nipple, back and forth, in
light teasing flicks that made her whimper with delight.

His other hand, he plunged into the masses of her
hair. He lifted his mouth from hers to say, "I've wanted
to do that all day." His fingers threaded through to her
scalp and then he combed through her curls. "Great
hair!" he muttered. "Great breasts! Great everything!"

It wasn't the most eloquent compliment Joanne had
ever received, but his words thrilled her as much as if
he'd composed a sonnet to her beauty.

She was having trouble breathing now and her knees
were shaky. Only her hands, clinging to the firm,
rounded muscles of Mike's back, helped keep her upright.

She needed to sit down—or better yet, lie down. And
not on the brickwork of her front porch. She stood on
tiptoe to bring her mouth as close to his ear as possible,
and murmured, "Why don't we go inside?"

He stiffened. His hands dropped away from her. He
swallowed and she saw the struggle he was undergoing
in the rapidly changing expression in his blue eyes.

But then he spoke—in tones that were so level, so
unemotional, that she could have wept: "I don't think
we'd better do that, Joanne."

A hot flush of embarrassment climbed her cheeks. "I
see. Well . . ." she murmured inanely.

She could have killed him for needing to explain. "It's
just that if I came in, I'm afraid we might end up making love," he said.

Exactly what she'd had in mind. She could feel her
flush deepening to the color of the bricks they stood
upon. If she could have found a way to sink through the
mortar between those bricks and disappear, she would

have done it. At least, she kept herself from saying anything silly this time. Instead, she said nothing at all.

Mike seemed to tower over her, virile, aroused; she could see the evidence of his desire distending the front of his trousers. But his voice was gentle, almost apologetic, as he finished, "And I never go to bed with a woman on the first date."

4

THE WAITER approached the table where Joanne sat with her best friend, Lindsay Reynolds. Sunday brunch was a tradition the two women maintained as best they could, and this patio restaurant was one of their favorite meeting spots.

It was cool and pleasant—or would have been pleasant if Joanne hadn't felt gnawed by self-recrimination.

"A cocktail for you ladies today?" The waiter, an older man with thin strands of gray hair carefully plastered across his bare scalp, balanced his pencil point against his order pad.

"A cup of hemlock would be nice," Joanne replied bitterly.

The waiter looked perplexed. "I beg your pardon?"

"Sorry. It was a joke. Iced tea, please."

When the waiter had gone, Joanne looked up to see Lindsay regard her quizzically. "Hemlock, huh? I take it your date wasn't all you'd hoped for."

Joanne groaned. "Hardly." She related the events of the evening she'd spent with Mike, even telling Lindsay that she had invited Mike in, expecting that the two of them would end up in bed—"Or on any other reasonably comfortable flat surface," she added wryly—but that he had refused.

"Oh, God, I felt like such a fool!" Joanne wailed.

The waiter brought their meals. Lindsay waited until he had departed to say, "So what are you going to do about it?"

Joanne picked up her fork and poked uninterestedly at her Spanish omelet. "Do? Well, I considered moving to Borneo, but on further reflection, I decided that won't be necessary. I'll probably never lay eyes on Mike Balthazar again, anyway."

Considering what had happened between them, she ought to feel glad that she wouldn't be encountering him. "Glad," however, was not how she would have described the emotion that laced through her at that thought. In fact, it felt remarkably like disappointment . . . regret. . . .

Lindsay took a bite of her crepe and then asked, "What about your pool? I thought you'd asked him to come up with a design for it."

Joanne covered her eyes with her free hand. "Oh, Lordy! I forgot about that. What am I going to do?"

"I have a suggestion." The brunette smiled. "It's a Joanne-type suggestion, so you *ought* to like it."

"What do you mean, 'a Joanne-type suggestion'?"

"You'll see. I suggest you—" Lindsay paused, obviously for dramatic effect "—go *talk* to him."

Joanne smiled. Lindsay was right. That *was* the kind of suggestion she would have offered to other people— or, in other circumstances, to herself. "Great idea! I can be embarrassed all over again!"

"Not necessarily." Lindsay speared a piece of melon and waved it for emphasis. "Listen, Joanne. For years I've heard you complain about the men you go out with. That they're pompous or stuffy or boring or grabby or—" she shrugged "—gay, like Warren."

"Well, they are . . . were."

"But I didn't hear you say any of those things about Mike."

"True. Because he's *not* boring or pompous or stuffy... or any of the rest."

"And there's another thing," Lindsay continued. "*You* couldn't see how you looked when you were talking about him, but I could."

"Humiliated? Mortified?" Joanne suggested.

Lindsay shook her head. "Not when you were telling me what Mike was like, how he reacted, how it felt dancing with him...."

Joanne bit her lower lip. "I really liked him. And he turned me on. A lot," she admitted in a quiet voice.

"And how many guys that you've been out with lately can you say *that* about?"

Joanne pretended to count, then shook her head. "None. Not in ages and ages and ages. Maybe never. But he's not interested."

"*He* didn't say that. All he said was that he doesn't go to bed with a woman on a first date."

"That's all he *said*," Joanne agreed. "But there was more to it than that. I don't think he really wanted to go out with me in the first place. I think I surprised him into it."

Lindsay frowned. "You're *sure* he was attracted to you?"

"Oh, yes," Joanne said confidently. Her certainty had nothing to do with vanity. She recognized chemistry when it happened. And there was chemistry between her and Mike Balthazar—no doubt about *that!*

"Then we're back to where we started. I think you ought to go talk to him," Lindsay advised. "At the very least, you'll clear the air. At the most—well, who knows?"

"Maybe he'll build my pool for me. I really did like his ideas." That was the very most she could hope for, she told herself. A wonderful swimming pool. She wouldn't think about other possibilities.

"Well, then . . . Go for it."

"Okay, I will." She was silent for a moment. "But what if he refuses to see me?"

Lindsay gave her an astonished glance. "Joanne Stephenson, I'm surprised at you. Is this the same woman who besieged the CEO of one of the biggest corporations in Southern California until he agreed to support her favorite charity? Is this the woman who lay in wait six evenings running for the president of a local bank so she could bully him into contributing to a scholarship fund for ghetto kids? Is this—"

Joanne lifted both hands. "Those times were different, Linds. I was doing it for a good cause."

"This is a good cause, too."

Was it? Joanne asked herself. Well, she supposed it was. To clear the air between her and Mike and to end up with a Balthazar pool. Surely those were worthy ends.

She took her napkin from her lap and put it on the table beside her untouched plate. "You're right. Okay. I'll do it. I'll go call and make an appointment to see Mike." She winked at Lindsay. "Under an assumed name, just in case. Maybe I'll use Reynolds, if you don't mind me borrowing it."

Lindsay gave an airy wave of her hand. "Be my guest!"

Joanne rose. She was halfway across the patio before she remembered and made an abrupt about-face.

Back at their table, she said, "I forgot. It's Sunday. His office is closed. I definitely need to keep this on a businesslike footing, so I'll call tomorrow."

IT WAS LATE the following morning. Fuming, Joanne closed the door behind the most recent applicant sent by the Elite Employment Agency. She strode over to the breakfast area and furiously punched the number into the phone. "It won't do," she said as soon as she was connected to Marilyn Burnham.

"I beg your pardon?" replied Ms. Burnham's penetrating voice.

"Excuse me," Joanne corrected with elaborate sarcasm, "I should have said, '*She* won't do.' Mrs. Plumb, I mean."

"I'm sorry you didn't find Mrs. Plumb satisfactory. What seemed to be the problem?"

"She talks. She was here fifteen minutes and I learned all about her migraines, her sciatica, and her postnasal drip. Not to mention her 'arthuritis.' The woman's a walking catalog of illnesses. If she were around here for very long, I'd start developing symptoms, too."

Ms. Burnham's sigh was a production number worthy of a Busby Berkeley musical. "I'll see what I can do, Ms. Stephenson."

"Please do," Joanne said crisply.

She hung up the phone. As satisfying as the conversation with Ms. Burnham had been, she was feeling the guilty unease that afflicted her when she hadn't done something she knew she ought to have done.

The thing that she hadn't done was telephone Mike Balthazar—and she hadn't done it yet because she was chicken.

She thought: Joanne Stephenson, chicken? *Hah!*

Drawing a deep breath, she picked up the phone and dialed.

MIKE LOOKED UP from a permit application he was filling out as Kitty trailed into his office. She put a memo slip down on his desk. "I just made an appointment for a Mrs. Reynolds to come see you tomorrow."

"See me here?" Mike asked, surprised.

Normally Mike or Bill called on potential clients at their homes. Since the office primarily existed as a place to do paperwork and for Kitty to answer calls, it was sparingly furnished—long on filing cabinets and short on comfortable chairs. The carpeting was dark brown industrial quality, and the walls were covered with imitation wood-grain paneling.

"That's what she wanted," Kitty explained. "Something about the house not being built yet, so she couldn't meet you there."

"Well, all right," Mike said reluctantly, reminding himself that this Mrs. Reynolds would be interested in the quality of the pools they built, not the office's interior decoration.

WEARING A FUCHSIA BIKINI, Joanne lay on the redwood deck behind her house. Again, she was practicing her Czech. Listening intently to the voice coming from the cassette tape, she slowly repeated the phrase, *"Servis V tomto hoteli je velmi nedobry."*

Then she had second thoughts. She couldn't imagine herself being rude enough to say, "The service in this hotel is very poor," even if it was. She was beginning to think she had made a very bad choice of language tapes.

She reached out and snapped off the cassette player. At least she'd learned some of the essential phrases she would need on her trip to Prague in the fall. She could order food, ask for directions and, most important, find out where the bathroom was in Czech.

She toweled down and went inside to check her answering machine.

The flashing light on the machine indicated she had several calls. Doug. He was thrilled to pieces that his golf trophies were still around and asked her to put them aside because he planned to pick them up sometime soon.

Since their divorce, she had grown quite fond of Doug. Now she was grateful to him—for having had a midlife crisis that had led him to take up with a younger woman, and in the process, freeing her.

Not that she exactly _enjoyed_ living alone. With the right man—one not as obsessive and disapproving as Doug had been—marriage, she supposed, could be quite pleasant.

The next message was from Warren, asking her to call him. She dialed his office number. When he answered, she announced, "Has anybody told you? The dollar has dipped, bonds have hit bottom, and the Dow-Jones is down three hundred and seventeen points."

"What?" he shrieked. "Who is this? Is this _true?_"

"It's a joke, Warren. It's me, Joanne, returning your call."

There was a gasp. Then Warren said severely, "Don't ever ever _ever_ do that again. And me just out of the sickbed, too." He paused, then asked, "How was the 'do' Friday night?"

She'd have been willing to bet that Warren had already heard all about it from some of their mutual

"I was afraid you wouldn't see me," she said, then hurried on before he could comment. "I wanted to say a couple of things I didn't get to say on Friday night. The main thing is, I want you to know that I'm really not promiscuous. I don't normally expect to go to bed with a man on a first date. Or *want* to, for that matter."

He tried not to let his astonishment show on his face. The last thing he would ever have expected was that she would refer to what had happened. Her candor was... He didn't know how to take it. And her mention of bed had brought back stirrings of the desire he'd felt for her.

His mouth dried up. All he could manage was a rusty-sounding "I know."

"Do you?" She gave a doubtful shake of her head. "I'm not sure if you do, Mike."

He wasn't sure if he did, either. The life-style she led, the people she associated with... Her ways were bound to be different from his.

He said slowly, "I suppose it's okay for other people these days, but I'm not the kind to have a one-night stand."

Horror struck, Joanne stared at him. Was *that* what he thought she had had in mind? "Neither am I. Heavens, no!"

"You didn't let me finish." He glanced down at the desk. "I know it makes me sound out of step with the times, but—" he shrugged "—so be it. I'm not interested in a . . . a fling, either. A short-term affair. Whatever you want to call it."

"Amazing," Joanne breathed.

Mike shifted uncomfortably. She could see the muscles in his forearm clench.

"I'm not criticizing," she continued hurriedly. "As a matter of fact, I think that's admirable. It's just unusual, these days."

He didn't say anything, but he relaxed visibly—enough that she decided she could risk teasing him. Straight-faced, she asked, "So tell me, Mike, are you holding out for marriage? Or is an engagement enough for you?"

For a moment, his face was stony. The first day they'd met, he'd had a sense of humor. It must still be in there somewhere, she thought desperately.

And it was. A short burst of staccato laughter erupted from his chest. Leaning back in his chair, his strong, muscular hands braced against the desk, he protested, "Oh, come on! Give me a break! I'm not *that* old-fashioned."

Joanne smiled. Leaning forward, he continued, "I just think there ought to be the *possibility* of a long-term relationship developing before two people go to bed with each other."

It took a moment for his words to sink in and when they did, her smile faded and died. She wasn't dumb. She could see the implications of his statement as if they'd been blazoned on the office wall behind him. The *possibility* of a relationship. That was all he insisted upon. And that meant that with her, he considered *that impossible.*

"I see," she said slowly. "And you don't think that you and I ever could . . ." She let her voice trail away.

He shook his head. It was a no-nonsense head shake, accompanied by a firm no-nonsense expression. He was a perfect illustration of a man with his mind made up. Joanne realized that there was no way on God's green earth that she was going to be able to change it.

So be it, she decided. She might as well accept the inevitable.

"Okay," she stated crisply. "I get the message."

He looked as if he might be going to apologize—or explain further, which would have been unbearable. So, before he could speak, Joanne went on rapidly, "Anyhow, now that that's out of the way and we understand each other, what about my pool?"

TEN DAYS LATER, Mike frowned at the watercolor drawing on his desk. She'd never go for it, he thought unhappily. Not being a trained artist like those landscape architects, he simply hadn't been able to translate his mental vision onto paper. Oh, here and there he had managed suggestions of it. But it wasn't good enough.

And there wasn't enough time for him to start again. Joanne Stephenson was due at his office any minute now. He had offered to bring the plans and sketches by her house, but she had said she'd be in the area and would stop by.

The air conditioner in the window was rattling away, so Mike didn't hear the door open. When Kitty said, "Ms. *Stephenson*'s here, Mike," he was caught off guard.

Again, Joanne looked like a businesswoman, wearing a conservative peach-colored dress with hose and high heels. She must have been outdoors fairly recently because her skin was flushed and she was sweating.

No, not sweating, he corrected, remembering an old-fashioned saying of his grandmother's: "Horses sweat. Gentlemen perspire. Ladies . . . glow." So Joanne glowed. In fact, there *was* a kind of glow about her; of course there always was. Or maybe it was just something about her that made him feel that way.

"Have a seat," he told her. "Would you like something to drink? I've got some soda in the fridge."

Joanne gave a faint grimace. She felt limp, sticky and hot. "It shows, does it?" She fanned her face with her hand. "I'd love a cola."

Mike rose. Joanne noticed how fresh he looked in beige slacks with a tan, short-sleeved shirt that looked as if it had emerged from a laundry package seconds before.

He opened a closet door. Inside was a pint-size refrigerator.

"All the comforts of home," she murmured.

"Not quite *all*."

He came out of the closet holding a frosty can, which he handed to her. Joanne took it gratefully. Before opening it, she held it against her cheek for a moment. "That feels great. It's a terrible day to be outdoors for very long."

Mike sat down behind his desk, then popped the tab on his own soft drink. "Golf?" he asked curiously. "Or tennis?"

"Neither one. Believe me, if I'd had a choice, I would have stayed indoors." She paused. "Or in a pool. If I had a pool . . ." She looked meaningfully at the rolled-up drawings on Mike's desk.

Rather than unrolling them, he leaned forward. It was none of his business, Mike told himself. But his curiosity was aroused. He'd spent plenty of days as hot as this one out in the sun. But what would make a rich woman like Joanne Stephenson do that?

"So, what *were* you doing outdoors?"

"I was at the zoo."

"The zoo?"

She nodded. "Yep. I'm a docent there."

"A docent?" He'd heard the word, but he had always associated it with universities and ceremonial occasions.

"Uh-huh. Recently, I've been giving the grand tour to groups of kids from day camps. I talk about the different animals, where they come from, how they live in the wild." She smiled. "Just doing my bit for ecological awareness."

"How often do you do this?"

"Once a week. I may not exactly love every minute of it when it's as hot as it's been today, but it's a *lot* more fun than some of the other things I do."

"Other things?"

Joanne looked down. Perhaps she shouldn't remind him. "Well, things like organize the fund-raiser we went to." Quickly she went on, "It made a *lot* of money, by the way."

"Good. I'm glad to hear it. So, what else do you do?"

"Oh, this and that."

"For instance?"

She hesitated, then said, "Well, there's the World Wildlife Fund. Twice a year, they put on a fair, a bazaar . . . whatever you want to call it." She fluttered her hand across the lower part of her face, as if drawing a veil. "Behold, Madam Mysteria," she intoned dramatically. "Knows all, tells all." She laughed. "I tell fortunes with the tarot cards."

"Do you believe in that stuff?" he asked curiously.

"Madam Mysteria does, absolutely. Myself—" she shrugged "I'm more a skeptic. But it's fun to do."

"Okay. What else?"

She was very good at "Strong-arming," as Lindsay put it, contributions out of corporations. But she couldn't imagine that that would interest Mike.

She shrugged. "Three afternoons a week, I work in a thrift shop."

"For charity?"

"Uh-huh. The profits go to an organization that supplies guide dogs to the blind."

"Anything else?"

He was looking at her with admiration, which made her feel uncomfortable. She wanted to explain that it wasn't virtue or altruism that made her do the things she did. The things she did were . . . just the things she did, the same way Mike Balthazar built swimming pools. And they were also the way she paid back her good fortune.

"Not really. Well, just odds and ends." An excellent time to change the subject, she decided. She gestured at the papers on his desk. "Are those for my pool?"

He nodded, but made no move to unroll them.

"I really want to get moving with this thing," she told him. "I'm getting to the point where I'd settle for one of those plastic pools, if it was deep enough to get wet in." She passed the back of her hand across her forehead and said weakly, "I can't go on like this much longer."

Mike brought his elbows up and rested them on the desk. "You do know that even if you like the design I've come up with and decide to go ahead right away, it's going to take time. There are soil samples to be taken, permits to be applied for, crews to be scheduled. Putting a pool in doesn't happen overnight."

"Yes, I understand. All the more reason why I'd like to get started as soon as possible." Again she glanced at the papers on his desk. "May I see?"

Mike repressed a sigh. He couldn't stall any longer. He would just have to steel himself for the look of disappointment in her eyes when she saw what he had come up with.

He nodded and turned the rolled drawing so that, spread out, it would be facing her. "I have to warn you I'm no artist. This is just a rough sketch. It doesn't really do it justice."

Holding one end down, he unrolled the other, then held the edges of the drawing so she could see.

Joanne gazed down at his watercolor sketch. The setting was her backyard, with the slope of the hillside rising behind and the little stream running onto the property. But now the stream appeared to feed a woodland pool whose shape was roughly oval. Mossy stones, not cement or tile, surrounded it. A pebbled path curved toward the redwood deck.

Joanne looked up and met Mike's gaze. "It's beautiful," she breathed.

"Do you really think so?"

"It's gorgeous! It's wonderful!"

Mike couldn't contain the broad grin that spread across his face. Her excitement was contagious. And gratifying.

Without thinking, he rose and went around behind Joanne. Leaning over her shoulder, he pointed. "Here's where we'll conceal the pool machinery, behind this mound. And here, this little section—I know you probably can't tell from this drawing—this is actually the spa."

"I could tell," she insisted. "You did a beautiful job with this, Mike. I'm really impressed."

He could feel himself coloring slightly. Blushing! *How ridiculous!*

He pointed toward the back of the lot. "This I'm not sure of. There may have to be a retaining wall going up the hillside."

"Yes, fine," Joanne agreed.

"And I'm not sure about some of the plantings. I'm not a garden designer. If you decide to do it this way, then I'll need to find out what grows well in that soil and exposure."

"Yes. Fine. Whatever. Those are all details we can work out later. The main thing is that it's fabulous and I want it. Just one thing . . ." She swiveled to smile up at him. "You haven't said how much."

Mike had bent over her shoulder to point at the plans in her lap, so his face was fairly close to hers. And when she turned her head toward him and gave him a direct, wide-eyed look, his breath stalled in his chest. Her eyes were so big, so blue. Excited and pleased and happy— because of something *he*'d done—she looked about seventeen. Her skin was dewy, her lips slightly parted . . . and he wanted to kiss her so much that it hurt.

He'd better slam the brakes on *those* feelings. Abruptly, he straightened.

"Mike?"

"What?"

"How much are we taking about?" she repeated.

He backed up a step and snapped out the *very* large sum.

She heard the figure without recoiling. "Fine. Let's do it."

Mike's lower jaw dropped. "You mean it? Just like that?"

"Of course, I mean it." She extended her hand. "Let's shake on it."

He ignored her outstretched hand and hurried back around to his side of the desk. Only a fool would deliberately involve himself in skin-to-skin contact with her at a moment when his defenses had plummeted to a new low.

Joanne concealed a secret smile as Mike retreated from her. She *was* rather sorry that he wouldn't shake hands with her today. She still remembered their first handshake. Remembered? It was engraved on her flesh, along with each of Mike's kisses and every single caress. But she couldn't help feeling that it was a good sign that he didn't have the nerve to shake hands with her today. A very good sign that he wasn't anywhere near as impervious to her as he might like to pretend.

She looked closely at him. His pupils were large and he was carefully not looking at her—signs that the chemistry between them was still there for him, just as it was still there for her. Simply looking at him made her feel warm and . . . excited.

They were bound to see each other fairly often while her pool was being built.

She couldn't conceal her smile. "I'm so pleased about this, Mike," she said. "I just can't tell you how pleased I really am."

5

JOANNE STRETCHED the phone cord to its limit, then leaned forward to open the front door of her house with one hand. On her doorstep stood Warren Frostine in an elegant three-piece navy suit. Warren had sable hair, which Joanne suspected retained its hue with help from a bottle; his closely trimmed mustache and beard had reached the salt-and-pepper stage.

"Still no housekeeper, I see." He glanced at the cord stretching behind her all the way through the big open space to the back of the house. "And why not get a cordless phone?"

"I have a cordless phone," Joanne replied. She was on hold and had been on hold for quite some time. A more suspicious person than she might have concluded that Marilyn Burnham of the Elite Employment Agency was trying to avoid speaking with her.

Warren cocked his head to one side. "Funny, it doesn't look cordless to me."

"Not *this* one," Joanne said witheringly. Still on hold, she turned and led Warren toward the back of the house.

"So, why don't you use it, then?" he asked as he followed her.

"Because it kept making calls on its own."

Warren nodded wisely. "It's on the wrong frequency. All you have to do is take it back where you bought it and have them change the frequency for you."

"I know that, Warren."

"Well, then?"

"I simply haven't had the time." Late July and early August seemed to be everyone's choice for vacations. Joanne had been filling in for other people, working extra days at the zoo and at the thrift shop. Furthermore, several organizations she supported were beginning to plan fall fund-raising activities, so as well, there had been more than the usual number of meetings.

One kind of meeting she *hadn't* had during the past week was a face-to-face meeting with Mike Balthazar. She had talked to him on the phone exactly once during the past seven days. He had assured her that things were proceeding as they should and she had had to be content with that.

Suddenly the insipid music that had been playing in her left ear stopped. A voice Joanne recognized as belonging to the receptionist at the Elite Employment Agency asked, "Are you still holding?"

"Yes, I am," Joanne said firmly, "and I mean to go on holding until I die of old age or Ms. Burnham does— whichever comes first. You might just mention that to your employer."

The receptionist sounded flustered. "Yes, I'll tell her. And I'm sorry you've been kept waiting, Ms. Stephenson."

During this last exchange, Warren had wandered off. He had a habit when in her house of strolling around a room, examining anything and everything. He was doing that now, charting a leisurely zigzag course back through the family room into the more formal living room area.

From the corner of her eye, Joanne noticed him bending over the polished burl-wood coffee table. He looked through the sheaf of brightly colored leaflets the travel agent had sent her, describing excursions in and around Prague. Joanne hadn't had a chance to look closely at them. Fortunately, there was no hurry. Her trip wasn't for months.

She returned her attention to the telephone as Marilyn Burnham's tones assailed her eardrums. "I'm dreadfully sorry to have kept you waiting, Ms. Stephenson. An emergency. You understand."

Joanne decided not to challenge her on this point. She had won the skirmish—no need to rub it in. "About your most recent applicant," she began.

Marilyn Burnham said tightly, "Yes, and what seems to be the problem with *this* one?"

"She drinks. Nine in the morning and she was reeking of it!"

Marilyn Burnham let out a shriek. "I *know* she drinks. She drinks like a fish. She's been fired from her last three jobs. And do you know what? I'm starting to think she has the right idea. I may take to drink myself."

Joanne ignored the last remark. "If you knew she drank, why did you send her to me?"

She made little sputtering sounds, then finally explained, "Because I've sent you every woman on our list who's even minimally qualified. You've rejected every single one."

"Every *woman* on your list?"

"Yes."

"Then maybe you'd better start sending me some men." Joanne took some satisfaction in banging the phone down.

Warren had wandered back into the breakfast area. "Ready to go?"

Joanne sighed. "No, not quite. I'm afraid I'll have to call Marilyn Burnham back. I let my tongue run away with me. If I don't cancel what I just said, she's likely to take me at my word."

"So?"

"And send me male applicants for a housekeeper's job?"

"Tsk, tsk," replied Warren. "I'm ashamed of you. And I thought you prided yourself on being so liberated. Besides, don't you ever watch television? Tony Danza does it on that show, whatever it is . . ."

"*Who's The Boss?*" Joanne supplied. "But that's television, not real life."

"But what would be wrong with having a male housekeeper? As long as he knows how to do the work, I mean." Warren waggled his eyebrows lasciviously. "There might even be some side benefits."

Joanne gave him a quelling glance. "Get your mind out of the gutter, Warren."

"Oh, very well," he said pettishly, then straightened his already impeccably straight tie. "But seriously, why not accept a male housekeeper if they have any?"

"They won't."

"You never know." Warren glanced at his watch. "Come, my sweet. The meeting starts at two and unless we hurry, we're going to have to positively gobble our lunch."

MIKE PUSHED OPEN the office door. He had just spent the afternoon talking to prospective clients. All over Southern California, it felt like. He was sure he'd spent a good three-quarters of the day on the freeway.

The window air conditioners in both the inner and outer offices were wheezing away and it was obvious

the noise had covered his arrival. Kitty wasn't at her
desk, but the door to the inner office was ajar and his
daughter-in-law's voice came through the opening loud
and clear. "Well, if you won't, then I *will*."

Bill's soft tenor responded, "Oh, no, Kitty, honey.
Please don't do that."

Mike's lips tightened. Why couldn't they keep their
arguments at home so he wouldn't have to overhear
them? He hated it that Bill sounded so weak and whiny,
as if he were pleading with his wife.

None of my business, he reminded himself.

"I'll do it, honest," Bill went on placatingly.

"When?"

Before Bill could answer, Mike cleared his throat—a
good loud throat-clearing to carry over the laboring air
conditioners.

There was a moment's silence and then Kitty called,
"Hi, Dad!" She stood in the doorway separating the two
offices. "Have a good day? I bet you're hot and thirsty."
As he walked past her into the inner room, she suggested, "Let me get you something cold to drink."

"That's very nice of you, Kitty."

She went to the closet, took a soft drink out of the
refrigerator and pressed the frosty can into Mike's
hand. Then she walked briskly to the door, where she
turned to direct a meaningful glance at her husband.
"I've got a few calls to make." She left the room, clos-
ing the door behind her.

Mike sat down behind his desk and popped the tab
on his soda can. Bill was still standing awkwardly
nearby. But before Mike could ask him what was up,
he picked up a filled-out contract form. "What's this
one?" He glanced at the top of the form. "Stephenson.
I don't remember anything about that one." He turned

to the last page and let out a low whistle. "Wow! That's going to be some job!"

"If she signs," Mike said, though he had no reason to think she wouldn't. He reminded himself that he needed to call Joanne, to tell her the contract was ready and ask her if she wanted him to bring it by or drop it in the mail. Regardless—assuming she *did* sign and the work went ahead—he'd be seeing her soon.

And what was *that* going to do to his hormones?

Bill looked down at the contract. "Why didn't you tell me about this, Dad?" he asked quietly.

"Tell you about it?" It was true he normally kept Bill up-to-date on possible or pending work—especially jobs the scope of this one. So why hadn't he even mentioned it to his son?

Dumb question, Mike thought. He knew exactly why. It was because of *her*, because of what had happened between them—and what *hadn't* happened.

And he sure couldn't explain all *that* to Bill. Defensively, he replied, "I didn't know I was supposed to report to you."

Bill flushed a dull red. "I thought we were supposed to be in business together. You make me tell *you* everything, every little detail of every job I'm involved in, and you don't bother to mention an enormous project like this one." He waved the contract for emphasis.

It was a different thing altogether, Mike told himself, struggling to control a surge of anger—anger he had a hunch was so quick to flare up because he knew he was wrong. "I ask you to tell me what's going on because you don't have the experience—yet—to know when there might be problems developing."

"No? When am I going to get the experience, then? I've worked in the business with you since I was a kid."

"You'll get there. It just takes time."

A tiny vein pulsed at the side of Bill's forehead. "How much time? Look, Dad, this is something I was going to say to you today, anyway." He drew a deep breath. "I think it's time you let me have more responsibility."

So that was what Kitty had been pushing Bill to do. Mike shook his head. How could he give the boy additional responsibility? He was still a kid. Hell, he couldn't even stand up to his own wife. "I told you. You're not ready. You're still making mistakes. Big ones. That estimate could have cost us a fortune."

The moment the words were out, Mike wished he could snatch them back. He had shown Bill the errors he'd made in the remodeling estimate, explaining as tactfully as he could where his son had miscalculated. He hadn't meant to rub it in again now.

Bill paled. In a slow, defeated voice, he admitted, "Yeah, I guess you're right. I guess I'm *not* ready. Kitty thought that—"

"Kitty!" Mike exclaimed, his anger flaring anew. It was *her* fault he'd had to hurt his son's feelings. If he was conscious that there was something illogical about blaming her for his own hasty words, he managed to thrust the idea aside. "I heard you two arguing when I walked in. Why do you let her push you around like that?"

Bill responded stiffly, "I'm working on it."

"What do you mean?"

The younger man's soft brown eyes, so like his mother's, were shuttered, concealing his expression. "Kitty and I—we've been seeing a marriage counselor."

Taken aback, Mike was silent. Once, he would have disapproved, maybe told his son that only yuppies went to shrinks. But if a counselor could help Kitty and Bill work out their problems . . .

In a level tone, he said, "That's probably a good idea."

"Yeah, I guess." His face still drawn, Bill moved toward the door.

Mike hated leaving it like that. He needed to make a peace offering. He said heartily, "Say, it's been a while since you and Kitty have come over for dinner. I haven't lost my touch with a barbecue. How about Sunday night?"

They often dropped in to swim during the summer months. Bill had swum like a fish since he was a baby, and Kitty seemed to enjoy it, too. And usually, when they stopped by, they'd bring a pizza or something. But it had been a while since he'd issued an actual invitation—and it was all he could think of to offer as an apology.

"Dinner?" Bill turned back with his hand on the knob. "I don't know, Dad. I'll have to ask Kitty and see what she says."

After the door closed, Mike heard their voices in the outer office, but they kept them low, so he couldn't hear what was said.

A few minutes later, the door opened. "Sunday's fine," Bill announced.

JOANNE'S PHONE RANG, and she picked it up.

"Ms. Stephenson? Mike Balthazar here."

Joanne stifled a sigh. He had kissed her and he couldn't even call her by her first name. "Yes . . ." She hesitated. If he was going to "Ms. Stephenson" her, then she'd reciprocate. "How are you, Mr. Balthazar? Any news on my swimming pool?"

"I wanted to let you know that the contract is ready. Shall I put it in the mail?"

"No, don't mail it. I'll come by your office tomorrow."

There was a moment's hesitation before he said, "You shouldn't have to do that. I could bring it by your place this evening, if you're going to be home."

Joanne smiled and chastised herself for it. There was nothing whatsoever for her to be gleeful about. Mike was coming by so she could sign the contract for her swimming pool. That was absolutely all. "That's great," she told him. "I'll give you the deposit tonight, too, so we can get started right away."

"A deposit tonight? That really won't be necessary. I'm sure you'll want to take some time to go over the terms of the agreement. You can give me the deposit check after you sign the contract."

"No," she said firmly.

"No?"

"No," she repeated. "I don't need any time. I'm going to sign tonight. I trust you, Mr. Balthazar. Even if I didn't, I'm sure there'd be a million loopholes in any contract that you could wriggle out of. And besides . . ." How many times did she have to tell the man that she was in a hurry? That she wanted a *pool*. That wasn't all she wanted from Mike Balthazar, of course, but it appeared to be all she was going to get. "I really want to get going on this thing as soon as possible."

His tone was slightly dry. "Yes, you've mentioned that before. All right, then. I'll bring it by this evening—if that's all right with you."

"This evening is just fine."

She hung up the phone and returned to her living room. The most recent applicant for the position as her housekeeper was sitting on her couch. "Now, tell me," she said, eyeing the young blond man with suspicion. "Just exactly why do you want this job?"

IT WAS NOT QUITE EIGHT o'clock when Mike rang the doorbell of Joanne's house. It smelled different here in the canyon, he realized. The chaparral climbing the hillside had a distinctive spicy scent and there had been few enough cars passing through that the natural aromas managed to prevail over gasoline fumes. He was inhaling deeply, enjoying the sense of being out of the city, when the door opened.

Standing there was a young man of approximately college age, whose perfect features and sun-bleached hair made him look like the quintessential California kid—the kind of kid who had never done a lick of work in his life, who spent his time surfing and cruising the Pacific Coast Highway in an expensive car.

And the kid obviously never *would* have to do any work, Mike reflected. Even though he could see nothing of Joanne in the boy's features, this had to be one of Joanne's sons, home on vacation.

Despite his disdain, he wanted to be friendly. He extended his hand. "Mike Balthazar. I'm going to be building a pool for your mother. Are you Robbie or..." He was surprised that the name of her eldest came instantly to his tongue, even more surprised when it took him only a moment to dredge up the name of her other son. He wouldn't have thought he would remember. "Or are you Jeff?" he inquired.

The young man grinned, his white teeth sparkling against his deeply tanned face. "Neither. I'm Gary, Ms. Stephenson's new housekeeper."

Mike tried not to show his surprise, but knew at once from the amusement on Gary's face that he had failed miserably. "Oh, uh, I see," he said.

"No," Gary countered forthrightly. "Probably you don't see, but it suits me and it suits the lady. So everybody's happy—okay?"

"Uh, yeah. Okay," Mike echoed, but not without a mental shake of his head. Having a full-time servant was bad enough, but a young *man*?

Clearly the lady could afford it, and if it made her life easier, then what business was it of his?

No business of his, he answered himself.

Except that it was just another demonstration of how wide the gulf was between them.

Gary ushered Mike into the living room, where he settled on the long oyster-colored couch he remembered seeing during his previous visit. Several folders lay on the burl-wood coffee table in front of him. Idly, he picked up the topmost one.

Printed in English, it was titled, "Pearls of Czech Gothic Art." He opened it to find, described in English, a half-day tour within the city of Prague.

He hastily put the brochure down when he heard footsteps. At first, he couldn't tell where the sound was coming from. Then he spotted Joanne coming down the stairs into the foyer. No businesslike outfit tonight—her lime-green, full-skirted sundress was cut midway across her breasts, showing some cleavage. Her hair was a seductive tumble around her face.

His mouth went dry.

"Hi, Mike," she said gaily as she came into the living room area. "Can I get you something to drink?"

He had to moisten his lips with his tongue before he could say, "Yes, thanks. That'd be great."

She reeled off a list, and he responded with the only thing he could remember from it, which was "Coffee," even though he realized the moment she'd started toward the back of the house that he'd much prefer a beer—something to cool him down.

Not that he had any reason to need a cooling drink. The windows were open to catch the breezes that drifted through the canyon, and the house was delightfully cool. No. The heat came from him, kindled the moment he looked at her smiling face, her luscious figure—and remembered.

She returned in a few moments carrying a tray. In addition to a steaming cup of coffee and a sugar bowl and creamer, she had brought two frosty bottles of beer. "I thought you might change your mind and want beer, after all," she explained.

"Uh . . . good thinking. Thanks." He took one of the bottles and removed the screw-off cap, then tilted up the bottle and swallowed deeply. He felt more in command of himself now. She had sat down a decent distance away on the oyster-colored couch.

The room darkened. Mike was still perfectly in control and taking his second swig of beer, when she learned over to snap on the lamp on the end table. Its golden glow made her hair look like a sunset.

His poetic notion surprised him. It wasn't like him to come up with a comparison like that.

He gave himself a mental shake and said the first thing that came into his head. "How come you didn't have your housekeeper get the drinks?"

"Because Gary has a class tonight. He's studying to be an accountant. That's one reason he wanted a job as a housekeeper," she told him. "He used to be a waiter, but he had trouble scheduling his work hours around the classes he's taking. Our deal is that he gets four nights a week off, and plenty of time to study during the day."

"And you don't mind him taking all that time off?"

"Mind? Heavens no." She rolled her eyes. "After the people I interviewed, Gary's an absolute treasure. Or at least, I think he's going to be. Today was his first day."

"I see," Mike said, although he wasn't certain he did.

"He smiles, you see," added Joanne. "And he's healthy as a horse and he doesn't drink. At least, he swears he doesn't and I believe him." She grinned. "Besides, he has terrific references."

"Uh, that's good."

"Yep. It sure is." She picked up her own beer bottle and swallowed, tipping her head back slightly. The line of her throat was as pure as a girl's. The skin revealed above the sundress looked smooth and satiny. And below the gathered top, there was the curve of her incredible breasts. He remembered the feel of them pressed against him and desire sprang up in him, as hot and fierce as if it had been only moments ago that they had touched.

He had to say something—anything to distract himself, to build a barrier between them—before he leaped up and grabbed her.

So he gestured at the brochure on the coffee table and asked, "You going there? Prague?"

"Uh-huh," Joanne answered.

"Why Prague?"

"Why not Prague?" she countered.

"I don't know. Just because there are a lot of other places I'd go first, if I were going to travel." He hesitated, then said slowly, "But you've probably *been* to those other places, haven't you?"

"It depends on what 'other places' you're talking about."

"Paris?"

"Uh-huh."

"Rome?"

She nodded.

"London?"

Again, a nod.

"Tokyo?"

She didn't nod this time, but she held up three fingers—and it wasn't because she was trying to start a game of charades, he figured.

"You've been to Tokyo *three* times?"

"Yep. Doug—my ex-husband—liked Japan." She let out a wry laugh. "Frankly, I think it was because he kept fantasizing about geisha girls, but I couldn't swear that was the reason."

He ignored her comment. This conversation was doing exactly what he had wanted it to do—remind him of the differences between them. *Prague, for God's sake!* "Where else?" he asked challengingly.

"Where else what? Oh, where else have I been?" She gave a little shrug. "Quite a few places, I guess."

He tried a few more cities and countries, then finally gave up. "So you've worked your way through the list and now you're going to Prague, is that it?"

Joanne looked at him questioningly. There was something going on here that she didn't understand. Not only did Mike seem to be angry with her because she was going to Prague, he seemed to be relishing that anger in some peculiar way.

This man is confusing! Or perhaps, she suddenly realized, very *confused.*

Unfortunately, she couldn't tell him the truth about why she wanted so much to go to Prague.

A picture formed in her mind of a middle-aged face that shone with kindness—Nanny Matusczek.

A Czech war refugee, she had cared for Joanne from babyhood through her first few years of elementary school. Joanne had depended on her much more than on her busy, social parents. Often, to amuse her, Nanny had told Joanne about Prague, her native city. "The Golden City," she had called it, describing butter-yellow buildings gleaming in the sunlight.

It was then that Joanne had determined to go to Prague someday. Soon she would finally visit the "Golden City"—as a memorial and a tribute to the long-dead woman who had given her so much love.

But she simply couldn't explain that to Mike. Her childhood attachment to Nanny Matusczek—instead of to her distant parents—was almost pathetic. Joanne absolutely refused to be pathetic.

Instead, she said, "When I was a kid, I . . . I knew a woman who had come from Prague. She used to talk about it. She made it sound like a cross between Disneyland and the Taj Mahal. I've always longed to go there. But I let other people—Doug, for instance, and then, after my divorce, friends I traveled with—decide where we should go. So this trip is going to be a dream come true for me."

Mike looked at her quizzically. She sounded as if this was something she'd been wishing and waiting for for a long time. He couldn't imagine she had many dreams she had to wait for. Mostly, if she wanted something, she probably just went out and bought it.

That reminded him of the reason for his visit. He picked up his briefcase from the floor beside the couch. After opening it on the table in front of him, he extracted the contract. "It's just the way we discussed," he began.

He half rose and leaned toward her, extending the contract. As she took the document from him, her fingers brushed his. It was the briefest of contacts, but for an awful moment, Mike was undone all over again. All that anger he'd built, all that sense of removal from her, swept away by a moment's touch.

He pulled back from her as if he'd been burned. And while she glanced through the pages of the contract, as he insisted she do before signing, he concentrated very hard on that leaflet and thought, *Prague, for God's sake!* over and over and over again.

But the danger wasn't entirely over. There were two more perilous moments when they touched—once when he handed her a pen and again when he took back his copy of the contract and the check she'd written.

Finally, he was out of there—out of her house and on his way home, carrying with him the sense that he'd had an extremely narrow escape.

FEELING STRANGELY BEREFT, Joanne wandered into the kitchen where she found Gary back from class, making himself a pot of tea.

He turned and gave her a sympathetic look as she sauntered into the room. "Want a cup?" he asked. When she shook her head, he said, "You sure? You look like you could use it."

She hadn't bargained on a housekeeper who could read her mind. What *was* in her mind, anyway? A sense of deprivation, of loss, of . . . Could it be loneliness?

"No, I'm fine," she insisted. She went over to the bank of cupboards and opened one door, then another. She hoped Gary wouldn't ask her what she was looking for, because if he did, she had no idea what she would tell him.

But Gary merely took his teacup to the kitchen table and sat down. After a few moments of silence, he remarked, "Seems like a nice guy."

Joanne frowned. "Who? Oh, you mean Mike."

"Yeah. Mike." He stirred the steaming liquid in his cup. "You two have a fight or something?"

"No." You couldn't fight unless you had a relationship, and what she and Mike Balthazar had was ... nothing. Except that he was going to build a pool for her. But that was absolutely all there was to it.

And maybe, just maybe, she grudgingly admitted to herself, that was the very reason why she felt so rotten.

"GREAT DINNER, DAD." Bill pushed his chair back from the table. "Wasn't that great, hon?" He smiled at his wife.

"Very nice," Kitty agreed. She stood and began stacking plates.

"You don't have to do that," Mike protested. As a widower for the last four years, he'd learned to take care of things like that himself. In fact, he'd discovered that there were many household chores that Mary had always done that he actually enjoyed doing.

"I'll just take a few things out to the kitchen," Kitty said.

"So what's on for next week?" Bill asked as the swinging door shut behind his wife.

Mike felt something tighten deep inside himself. "We start the Stephenson job tomorrow."

"Oh. She must have signed the contract, then. That's great, Dad."

Mike shot his son a glance. He'd meant to tell Bill that the contract was signed, and that the job was due to start the following week. But again, his urge to keep everything to do with Joanne Stephenson to himself had interfered. What he ought to do now, was turn day-to-day supervision of some of the more mundane facets of the job over to his son.

His mental response was instinctive and immediate: *Like hell, I'll turn it over to Bill!*

An instant later, his son inquired, "Anything you need me to do for that one, Dad? Want me to supervise the excavation?"

"Nope," Mike replied. "I'll take care of it."

AN HOUR LATER, he watched them go, watched his son put his arm around his wife's waist as they walked down the front walk toward their car. The marriage counseling must be helping. They hadn't argued at all tonight.

Oddly enough, he actually found himself feeling envious of Kitty and Bill as he turned and went inside the house.

He wandered back to the kitchen. It was spic-and-span. The kids had insisted on helping him clean up. Then he detoured into the family room. He walked over to the TV and flipped it on. A repulsive game-show host leered at him. Mike flipped the TV off again.

He needed to be out, he decided. With people. He thrust aside the image that sprang to his mind of the person that he genuinely wanted to be with tonight: a pert nose and bright blue eyes, framed by that spectacular hair.

He left the house. A few minutes later, he found himself driving down a familiar street. A neon sign, Dyna-bowl, lit up the night. He didn't feel like bowling, but maybe he'd stop in at the bar in the bowling alley and have a beer or two. There was even a chance that somebody he knew would be there—somebody he could talk to.

And there *was* somebody he knew in the bar, back in a dim corner. Good, thought Mike, as he spotted Al MacPherson's balding dome. Al, a member of the same bowling league Mike belonged to, was recently divorced. He would be bound to be happy to have some company.

And then Mike saw that Al already had company. At the secluded corner table, the heavyset man was sitting cozily close to a slim brunette. Wasn't it only a few weeks ago that Al had been complaining about how lonely he was?

Something had obviously changed.

And how! As Mike watched, the brunette leaned toward his friend and planted a big sloppy kiss on good old Al's lips.

Mike quickly left the bar. Not only did he not want to horn in, the last thing he needed tonight was more couple stuff. It seemed as if everyone in the whole wide world had someone except him.

6

THE DEAFENING ROAR of the yellow tractor shovel blotted out everything else. Mike stood on the redwood deck behind Joanne's house and watched as the jaws of the machine took the first bite out of the earth. He always got a kick out of this moment at the beginning of a job. And this time, the first gobble of the machine inside the boundaries of the pool meant more than usual, since it was *his* design that would gradually come to life.

Assuming, that was, that Joanne got what she was paying for and he didn't screw something up royally along the way.

A STEMMED GLASS in each hand, Joanne stomped loudly on the redwood decking as she came up behind Mike. She didn't want to scare the life out of the man when she suddenly materialized at his side. No ordinary footsteps were going to penetrate the thunderous noise of the bulldozer, which was making a hearty breakfast of her backyard.

Either he had heard her approach, or he had nerves of steel, for when she touched the rim of a glass to his upper arm, he didn't jump, only veered around and smiled. He looked down at the bubbles rising in the champagne and mouthed something Joanne couldn't hear.

"What?"

He raised his voice. "Champagne? In the morning?"

"Sure!" Joanne shouted back at him. "Why not? When there's a reason to celebrate, it doesn't matter what time it is."

He shrugged and took the glass she offered him.

Only yards away, half a dozen men attended to their jobs. But as Mike lifted his glass to clink against Joanne's, it seemed to him as if the two of them were alone. The noise of the dozer created an illusory curtain of privacy.

Eye contact. As she stared into Mike's eyes, Joanne thought how strange it was that sometimes the meeting of eyes could be more intimate than a caress. Eyes were supposed to be windows to the soul.... If that was true, then her soul and Mike's were doing some heavy communicating.

The tractor shovel roared back toward the marked-out shape of the pool, then dipped its jaw for another bite.

Mike took a swallow of champagne. He couldn't seem to stop staring at Joanne. Her shoulder was only inches from his arm. He could sense her warmth, her softness.

Despite the odor of soil swirling up from the earth, Mike inhaled another fragrance, one that was sweet and spicy—and intoxicatingly female. That scent and the champagne mingled in his blood, annihilating his common sense. He blurted out, "Want to go out this weekend?"

The bulldozer roared and Joanne pointed at her ear, shaking her head in incomprehension.

Mike raised his voice, "Want to go out—"

At that moment, the tractor's engine shut down.

Jack Johanson, the tractor driver, looked over at Mike from his seat on the vehicle. He was a big beefy man, with dragon tattoos on both forearms. "We hit something, Mike. Might be a pipe," he called out.

There weren't supposed to be any water or gas lines within the area of excavation, but occasionally things weren't as they were supposed to be on city plans and maps.

"I'll check it out," Mike called back, stepping forward before any of the men closer to the pipe could get there ahead of him. He figured this was a reprieve—a moment to consider whether he *really* wanted to do what he had been about to do—ask Joanne Stephenson for a date.

He got to the hole in the earth and took a hand shovel from one of the crew. A moment later, he told Jack, "It's a pipe, all right, but it's not connected to anything." It could be from an old irrigation system. He had run into pipe like this before.

Using hand shovels, he and two of the other men loosened it so that the machine's jaws ought to be able to lift it free. Mike stepped back, waving the high sign to Jack. The dozer roared to life and Mike gave his shovel back to the man he'd borrowed it from, then returned to the deck.

Joanne was still standing where he'd left her. She looked up at him, started to speak, then smiled and again pointed to her ear. Finally she gestured with her head in the direction of the house.

Mike followed her across the deck with reluctant steps, trying to decide what he was going to do now. Repeat his invitation? Or make up something else entirely and claim that that was what he'd been going to say?

She pushed open the sliding-glass door and preceded him inside. Mike followed her and shut the door, muting the snarl of the earth mover. He could even hear the hum of the air conditioning and, from upstairs, the purr of a vacuum cleaner. Gary, doing his job, Mike guessed.

Joanne looked up at him. She twirled her half-empty champagne glass between her slender fingers. "Now, what was it you were asking me, Mike?"

Sirens and alarms went off in Mike's mind, all blaring the same message: *It's not too late! It's not too late! Save yourself while you can!*

But another treacherous part of his mind suggested that he was making a big deal out of nothing. He wasn't proposing marriage here. All he was doing was asking a woman out on a date.

He glanced down at the red tile floor, then raised his gaze to her face. "I was just wondering if maybe you'd like to do something some night this weekend. Dinner. A movie, maybe."

Joanne blinked, then quickly concealed her astonishment. She was almost tempted to ask him why, after all this time, he had changed his mind. But she didn't know whether he *had* changed his mind, she reminded herself. Deep down, he still might believe that the two of them could never have a relationship. But then, why would he ask her out?

Deciding not to torment herself with questions, she smiled up at him. "That sounds very nice, Mike. I'd like that."

"Saturday?" Mike questioned.

Joanne calculated quickly. Saturday evening, she was supposed to go to an art exhibit with Warren. He would forgive her for begging off, she decided. And if he *didn't* forgive her, it was just too damn bad. This was one invitation she wasn't declining for anything short of a national emergency.

"Saturday will be fine," she said. "Just fine."

Understatement, she thought.

"YOU COULD HAVE KNOCKED me over with a feather," Joanne reported later by phone to Lindsay. "I mean, the *last* thing I expected was for Mike to ask me out."

"How do you feel about it?" Lindsay asked.

Joanne didn't have to ponder at all. "Excited. Thrilled. Happy. Apprehensive. Nervous. Your basic sixteen-year-old idiot . . . again."

"You really *do* like this guy a lot," Lindsay observed.

"Yeah," Joanne agreed. "I guess I do."

HER ARMS LADEN with grocery bags, Joanne hurried through the big room to the back of the house. Mike's van was parked on the street. She hadn't seen him all week. According to Gary, he had been at her house a lot, supervising the work of his crews, but she had hardly been home.

With her foot, she pushed open the swinging door leading to the kitchen. Gary stood at the sink, washing lettuce for a salad. When he saw Joanne, he dropped the wet leaves into a bowl and hurried to take the shopping bags out of her arms. "Sorry, I didn't hear you come in."

Although the yellow bulldozer had done its work and the noise level drastically reduced, the backyard was a flurry of activity today. It was steel day—the day when men in hard hats bent and shaped steel reinforcing rods against the floor and walls of the gigantic hole behind Joanne's house.

She looked through the kitchen window. Three men were carrying long round steel rods to the edge of the excavation. None of them was Mike. Even with a hard hat on and at a considerable distance, he would be immediately recognizable to her, with his sturdy shoulders, rounded biceps, trim waist and hips.

"Uh, Joanne . . ." Gary was unpacking the grocery bags she'd brought in. "Did you get the fresh basil for the pesto sauce?"

"Oh, shoot! I forgot!" She had insisted upon doing the shopping herself because Robbie was coming home for a visit. As she had explained to Gary, "I'll only remember what he likes to eat when I see it on the shelves."

"It's okay," Gary assured her. "I have to go out later, anyway." He delved into the bag. "Oh, good! You remembered the pine nuts." Next, he held up a package with cartoon characters on the front. "Cocoa Marshmallow Sugar Crunch cereal. Does Robbie really *eat* this stuff?"

"As of a couple of months ago, he did." She shrugged. "After eating camp food for the last couple of months, he'll probably be grateful for anything." As she spoke, her gaze drifted back to the window. Where *was* Mike? Or had one of the other men driven his van today?

Gary gave her an acute glance. "He's in the hole, Joanne."

She didn't even try to pretend not to know who he was talking about. "Thanks. Is it okay to go out there, or do they yell at you?"

Gary shrugged. "Dunno."

"Why, those poor men," she said with exaggerated concern. "It's *so* hot out there today. I bet they'd love some iced tea."

In the end, she decided to carry out not only tea, but sodas and a few beers. Not that she wanted to encourage drinking while they were working on her pool, but these were construction workers, not a bunch of white-gloved elderly ladies.

She was halfway across the deck when one of the men spotted her and her burden. "Whooee! All right, lady!" he called, drawing the attention of the others.

A moment later, Mike climbed up out of the hole in the ground. As Joanne had thought she would, she recognized him the instant his hard-hatted head appeared above the rim.

A few minutes later, having downed half a glass of iced tea in one swallow, he drew her aside. "That was nice of you," he said, his appreciative gaze locked on her face.

"No big deal," she replied, meaning it. If ever a gesture had been for selfish reasons, it was this one. She had wanted to see Mike. Just standing near him made her heart accelerate, and spurts of adrenaline made her feel especially alive.

"About tomorrow night . . ." she ventured.

"Problem?"

At the sound of his voice, Joanne's excitement dimmed. He almost sounded hopeful, as if, on some level at least, he would be glad if something had come up to prevent them going out.

But if that was true, then why had he asked her out in the first place? She certainly hadn't strong-armed him into it this time.

The man was clearly ambivalent. And that just might be the understatement of the century: Every time he looked at her, she saw a spark of desire kindle in his eyes and yet . . . if she were to cancel their date, she felt that some part of him would leap up and click its heels together in celebration and relief.

"No. No problem," she told him, deciding there was no way she was going to let him off the hook. "I was just wondering how I ought to dress."

"Oh, casual," Mike said promptly. He had considered taking her some place fancy—the kind of place that she must go to with her friends. But he had decided that there was no way he could compete at their game; so he would just play his own game. He hesitated. "And you might want to bring a bathing suit."

Joanne's eyes lit up. "A swim?" she prompted rapturously.

"If you want."

"I want. More than you know." It would still be weeks until her own pool was completed; she was resigned to that now. "Anything else I should bring?" she asked. Where was this swim going to be? she wondered. His place?

"An appetite. You're dealing with a great barbecue chef here."

His place!

Well, all right! thought Joanne. It looked as if the man was finally beginning to see the light.

MIKE RANG THE DOORBELL, expecting the door to be opened by Gary—whom Mike had come to like. But unless the young man who stood there had dyed his hair and had plastic surgery since Mike had seen him the day before, it wasn't Gary.

This time, it *had* to be one of Joanne's sons. His freckles and carrot hair labeled him as her offspring.

"Robbie?" Mike ventured, because a while ago Joanne had mentioned being sad that she wouldn't be seeing Jeff for ages and ages. Robbie, however, was expected to visit for a couple of weeks in August.

The young man nodded.

"I'm Mike—" Mike began.

"Mike Balthazar," Robbie finished for him.

"Right. I'm . . ." He wasn't sure what he was going to say. Probably something about being the contractor for the swimming pool. He had no idea how Joanne's son would feel about her dating him, a blue-collar guy who'd never even been to college. Look at the way Joanne's snooty friends had reacted.

But before he could make up his mind how to identify himself, Robbie again finished his sentence for him. "A friend of Mom's," he said. "Yeah, I know. She was just telling me about you." His expression was pleasant, as if whatever Joanne had told him about Mike had predisposed her son to view him in a kindly light.

"Come on in." As he stepped back into the foyer, leaving room for Mike to enter, Robbie glanced up the stairs. In a lowered voice, he confided, "Mom's primping. Don't tell her I said that, okay? But I'll be willing to bet she'll be a while. Want a beer?"

"I, uh . . ." He paused. "Sure."

He followed Robbie to the kitchen. "It's a pretty cool house, isn't it?" Robbie said conversationally. "I only saw it once before Mom bought it. She wanted to make sure that Jeff and me—Jeff's my brother—that we liked the place. I thought it was cool then. Now that Mom's got it fixed up, it's *really* cool."

He went to the refrigerator and opened it, then pulled out a beer can, which he handed to Mike. "Want a glass?"

Mike shook his head. "The can's fine."

Robbie got a soda for himself and sat down at the kitchen table, gesturing for Mike to join him. "It'll be even better when the pool gets in," Robbie went on. "I don't know how Mom's been getting along without her swims. That's practically her favorite thing, you know." He laughed. "Besides doing good, I mean. I'm always kidding her, telling her she ought to have been a fairy godmother by profession. She really gets a kick out of helping people."

"I've gotten that idea. She certainly works hard at it."

"She sure does." He looked speculatively at Mike. "Say, I've been wondering... Is it hard to get a contractor's license?"

"I guess it depends how you define 'hard,'" Mike answered. "You have to know your trade, get at least three years' experience working at it, and then take the licensing exam." He regarded the young man curiously. "Why do you want to know?"

"I've got to start thinking about what I want to do when I get out of college." He lowered his voice. "*If* I get out— I mean, if I graduate. My grades aren't all that great. I'm hanging in, you know, but pretty much by my fingernails. Anyway, sooner or later, I'm going to have to decide what I'm going to do 'when I grow up.'" He put the last phrase in self-conscious quotes. "And I thought about maybe something in the building trades. I *know* I don't want to be cooped up behind a desk all day long. I'd just hate that."

"The first thing you have to do is learn a trade," Mike advised. Most kids *he* knew learned from relatives or friends. He felt sorry for Robbie. "I'll tell you what. I'll get some information together on some apprenticeship programs and pass it on to you."

"Hey, thanks! That would be great!" Robbie hoisted his soft-drink can and Mike had to smile. The gesture was so like one his mother made—for instance, when they'd toasted the excavation of the pool.

He was about to give Robbie a few words of advice when the swinging door opened.

"I thought I might find you guys back here," said Joanne with a smile.

TWENTY MINUTES LATER, Mike pulled his car into the driveway of a small ranch-style home. It had a neatly manicured lawn out front, whose green Joanne admired enthusiastically and sincerely. One of the things she liked about her own new house—apart from the spacious airy rooms and the cool tile floors—was the fact that it had no conventional lawn. She didn't have to worry about keeping one as green as her neighbors'. But she had fought the battle in her day and she knew how difficult it could be in the Southern California climate.

She found it rather amusing that as Mike ushered her into his house, they were discussing fertilizer. He whisked her on through the living room, then down a hall past closed doors and into the kitchen. There he stopped touting the merits of steer manure and said, "You know...I never actually asked if it was okay with you to eat here. At my place, I mean."

"Yes, you did. Sort of," Joanne responded. "We talked about a swim and a barbecue. I figured you must mean coming to your house."

She glanced around the kitchen. The wallpaper was a pattern that had been popular some years back—small brown churns and country stools and milk buckets against a background of pale yellow. The stove and refrigerator were the bronze color that Joanne liked, but that you simply couldn't buy anymore. Apparently Mike hadn't redecorated since his wife died.

Suddenly Joanne was aware that she was here in the house Mike had shared with his wife—a woman whose name she didn't even know. She hadn't thought about that before. She wondered if Mike had.

Don't borrow trouble! she instructed herself firmly.

The kitchen door leading to the outside had a glass upper half. It wasn't even six o'clock and was still bright; the summer twilight would last for hours yet. Through the window set into the door, Joanne could see the aqua sparkle of . . . heaven.

One sort of heaven, she amended. Another sort could be provided by the strong arms of the man who stood, rather uncertainly, a few feet away. *If he chose.* Whether or not he would was something Joanne simply couldn't guess. And if it felt right to *her* when the time came, of course. But she had a hunch she knew how she would feel. . . .

A shiver rippled through her. Had it been visible? Would Mike guess the cause? She darted a glance at him, then said quickly, "Oh, look at that pool! I can hardly wait!"

He smiled. "Go ahead and change. The guest bathroom's right down that hall. Second door on the left." He pointed back down the hall through which they'd come.

Joanne followed his directions. The first door on the left, which she was reasonably certain led to the master bedroom, was shut. Just as well, because otherwise she'd have been mightily tempted to peek.

The bathroom was as impersonal as guest bathrooms tend to be—nothing revealed here about the owner of this house. She *wanted* him to be revealed to her—not only physically, but mentally.

She pulled on her suit—one of her more conservative models. At least, she had thought of it as conservative. But, now that she looked at herself in the mirror, the suit seemed rather more daring. It was black and dipped low in front between her breasts. There were hardly any bathing suits with high necklines available this season. She tugged the elastic down over her derriere, then turned sideways to the mirror, pulling her stomach in so hard that her hipbones stuck out.

She held her breath for a moment, then exhaled, resigned to seeing a tiny roundness of stomach reappear. She was as she was. Whatever was going to happen was going to happen; and there wasn't really a whole lot she could do about it.

STANDING AT THE SINK, running water over a head of lettuce for the salad, Mike heard bare feet on the linoleum and turned . . . and felt as if he'd taken a fist in his gut. Her black bathing suit offered a bountiful display of her physical endowments. She was lovely. God, those breasts, that narrow waist, the swell of her hips!

His heartbeat quickened and he surreptitiously put his free hand on the edge of the counter to steady himself. "Go ahead," he told her, gesturing with the lettuce at the door that led outside. "Enjoy yourself!"

"Aren't you going to swim?"

"Maybe later. I still have a few things to do to get the dinner ready."

"Like what?"

"Oh, nothing much," he said casually, trying not stare too obviously at her cleavage. "Just a salad to make and the potatoes to put in the oven."

"I'll help with the salad," Joanne offered. "I'm a whiz at salads. It's about all I *am* a whiz at in the kitchen. And then we can both swim."

He might have protested, but she had moved closer and taken the head of lettuce out of his hand. She smiled up at him. "I can do this. Honest."

"Oh, I believe you," he answered, moving away from her so he could regain his concentration.

Joanne smiled. She hadn't missed his response to her. She had seen his convulsive swallow and his gaze focusing on her chest. The only trouble was, his reaction had ignited hers.

She turned toward the sink so Mike wouldn't see the evidence that she was every bit as hot and bothered as he was. "How did you and Robbie get along?" she asked him.

"Just fine." Mike had already scrubbed the potatoes. Now he opened a drawer, searching for an aluminum nail to stick in each one to convey the oven heat through them evenly. "He seems like a nice kid."

"He is," Joanne said fondly.

Mike found the nails and stuck one in each potato. "He was talking about what he's going to do when he gets out of college." He decided not to bring up the question of Robbie's scholastic standing. If his mother knew he was doing poorly, she might not want to be reminded; if she didn't know, Mike didn't especially want to be the one to rat on the kid. His own grades in high school had been strictly in the adequate range. He had never made it as far as college.

Joanne turned to look at Mike with interest. "Really? Was it anything sensible? I mean," she elaborated before Mike could reply, "when we talked about his future a few years ago, he was going to be a major-league pitcher. Or a race-car driver. He couldn't decide which." She laughed. "I hope he's being more realistic about it now."

"I'd say he was. He was asking me about the building trades."

"Hmm . . ." Joanne paused in the middle of tearing apart a lettuce leaf, then nodded. "I like it. That would be good for Robbie. Especially if it was something he could do outdoors. He's always been happiest with the sun shining down on his head."

Mike started to say something, then thought better of it.

Joanne looked at him. "What? Don't you think he could do something like what you do? He's not the greatest in school, but he's not a dumb kid. Not really."

"I didn't think he was. I was just curious . . ." His voice trailed away.

"About what?"

Mike hesitated, then blurted, "About why he needs to work at all. You don't."

Joanne smiled. "Ah, but that's because my great-grandfather was an MCP."

"MCP? A male chauvinist pig?" Mike questioned.

"Yep . . . though I don't think the term had been invented back then."

"What do you mean?"

She sobered, realizing that meant being candid about *The Money.* Not a topic designed to draw her and Mike Balthazar closer together. "Oh . . . It's the terms of my great-grandfather's trust. Female descendants—presumably because they were considered to be unfit to earn a living—come into their shares at twenty. But the male children have to wait until they're thirty-five. Robbie and Jeff'll both have to work for a living." She paused, then explained, "I could divert some funds their way, of course. But I won't. Or not unless I think they really need help."

She bit her lip. An old grievance burst out of her. "It was really unfair of the old b— All the burden was put on the women, while the men get to run around leading normal lives."

Mike looked across the room, wondering if he'd heard her right. Was she really complaining about *having* money? He must have misheard or misinterpreted. Yet, he could have sworn . . .

"How's the salad going?" he asked, deciding to put the question aside for later consideration.

"Almost done."

"Then I think we're all set. The coals on the barbecue need some time, but there's nothing else that needs to be done at the moment."

"Time for that swim?" Joanne asked.

"Sure is." Mike jerked his head in the direction of the backyard. "You go ahead. I'll join you in a minute."

THE WATER FELT DELICIOUS. She had dived in and swum several quick laps. Now she held herself up with an arm on the coping while she caught her breath—or pretended to catch her breath. The truth was she didn't want to miss Mike's arrival.

The back door opened and there he was, clad in skimpy dark brown trunks. He was *perfect*. His legs were strongly muscled and sprinkled with dark hair.

But more important, his chest was broad and decorated with dark, wiry-looking hairs.

Joanne had no compunctions about glancing even lower on his body. She was no blushing virgin. The male anatomy was familiar to her...and in Mike's case, intensely interesting. She glimpsed a bulge, but before she could get a really good look, he dived into the pool.

For the life of him, Mike had no idea if it was accidental or deliberate that he came up near Joanne—near enough that as he kicked toward the surface, one of his feet struck smooth female flesh. He broke through the surface of the water, his hair streaming over his forehead, and asked with concern, "Did I hurt you?"

Joanne shook her head. "No, I'm fine."

He rested his arm on the coping next to hers. "But I'm sure I kicked you. Where did I get you?"

Joanne made an instant decision. Boldly she looked him full in the face. "I'm not telling. I guess you'll have to check me over for injuries."

He caught on, and obviously decided to play along. "That seems only fair," he said slowly.

He somersaulted underwater. Joanne's breath caught in her throat as she felt his hands circle her ankles, then slowly move upward, palpating her flesh, as if he really were examining her for broken bones. The result was incredibly sensual.

At her knees he left off and came up for air. "So far, everything checks out okay," he reported.

Her breathing was slightly unsteady. "So far," she countered implying doubt about the rest of her.

Treading water, he put his hands on her waist and squeezed gently. "Okay here," he said. Then he slowly smoothed his hands down her sides, over her hips. "Just *fine* here," he remarked with emphasis.

And then his eyelids hooded as his gaze fixed on her breasts. She didn't mean to do it. Her response was purely involuntary, but she couldn't help herself. Her back arched, lifting her rounded breasts which were now aching for his touch, above the surface of the water.

Mike's voice was husky. "Guess I'd better—"

His voice broke as he put his palm on the underside of her breast, then smoothed upward. Her nipple was already pebble hard—as much from the desire for Mike that had tormented her for weeks, as from the cold water. She let out a soft gasp as he rubbed his thumb over the rigid peak. The sound was stifled when his mouth came down on hers, hard and hungrily.

The heat and passion of his kiss exploded through her, consuming her. His tongue filled her mouth. She didn't retreat before his onslaught but instead responded, probe for probe. Her open mouth against his, she greedily took all he had to offer and returned it in kind.

Her free hand explored his chest, smoothing over the wet, flattened chest hair, pressing against the muscles beneath. He was strong. Solid. Male. And the taste and the feel of him were so exciting that her skin felt electric.

She had no idea who was responsible for what happened next—whether it was she who shrugged a shoulder or Mike who dislodged the strap of black cloth. But her bathing suit was sliding down and her left breast suddenly sprang free.

Mike groaned and eased her back so she was half floating, though still anchored by one arm on the edge of the pool. He gazed at her nakedness for an instant before he bent his head and took her nipple into his mouth, sucking deeply.

A shaft of liquid heat ran from the tip of her breast—where Mike's lips and tongue were dealing out delicious torment—to the very center of her body.

Her legs parted slightly, her hips restlessly moving in the water. Mike's tongue licked her nipple, sending exquisite sensations through her, and heightening the tension between her thighs.

Head back, she let out a soft moan of pleasure. And then she heard something. Or half heard—her ears were partly underwater. But she could have sworn there were voices.

"Hey, Dad!"

"Hi, it's us!"

The voices came from near the back door of the house, only a half-dozen yards away.

7

JOANNE MOVED FASTER than the speed of light—uprighting herself in the water, turning to hide her bared breast, yanking the bathing-suit strap back into place.

But she hadn't been quite fast enough, she realized, when she turned around again and saw the young man and woman staring at her with shocked expressions on their faces.

She'd seen the girl at Mike's office. His daughter-in-law, he had said. That meant that the equally horrified-looking young man must be Mike's son.

She threw Mike a look that was both helpless and apologetic.

He wasn't looking at her, but scowling at the newcomers. He put the flat of his hands on the coping, preparing to pull himself up out of the pool. Then he glanced down at his lower body and evidently changed his mind. Instead, he swam over to the edge of the pool nearest Kitty and Bill. Those *were* their names! she now remembered.

Though Mike kept his voice low, Joanne heard him say, "You two should have called before you came over."

Bill shifted uneasily from one foot to the other. "Well, I'm sorry, Dad. You've never expected us to call before. You always said we could just drop in anytime."

Mike was silent for a moment, obviously trying to come to grips with himself. Then he said judiciously, "That's true. My fault." Without getting out of the pool, he performed introductions.

Emily Post never covered this *situation* Joanne thought, giving Mike's son and daughter-in-law a *very* bright smile.

They made awkward small talk about her new pool. Then Bill glanced at his wife. "Kitty, hon, we'd better go."

After they'd left, Joanne looked over at Mike, who was still in the pool, with one arm up on the coping. "I'm sorry," she said, sympathizing with him. She knew how she would feel if it had been one of her boys who had seen his parent doing what she and Mike had been doing.

He turned toward her, lifting one hand to push the wet hair back from his face. "No. *I'm* sorry," he said. He moved toward her. "My fault. As Bill reminded me, I've always let the kids think they could just show up whenever they wanted to. I've never asked them to call first or let me know."

"You don't have to explain," Joanne told him. "I understand completely." The open invitation meant he must not make a habit of entertaining half-clothed women in his pool. How could she complain about *that?*

"Do you?" His eyes searched her face.

"Sure I do, Mike. Really, it's not such a big deal." She laughed ironically. What was the exposure of her naked breast to two total strangers?

"It's a big deal to me," he said in a husky voice.

His gaze was riveted on the shadow between her breasts. Her nipples tightened. She'd assumed that the interruption of Mike's son and daughter-in-law had spoiled the mood, but suddenly she realized that it wasn't spoiled after all.

"What we were doing when they showed up . . ." He gave a swift baffled-looking shake of his head. "It was . . . I was . . ."

He might not be very articulate, but that didn't mean she wasn't getting the message. Particularly since, as he spoke, he lifted his hand to her waist. Beneath the water, his palm and fingers looked wavy and insubstantial, but his touch was firm, definite, possessive. Tantalizingly, he smoothed his hand upward over her midriff, so that once again, he cupped her breast.

"You are so beautiful," he murmured, and now his voice was hoarse, cracking with emotion. "And I want to make love with you, more than I can tell you."

Her own voice emerged thick with longing. "I want to make love with you, too, Mike."

She moved even closer to him, fluttering her feet to keep herself upright in the water. Then she lifted both hands and placed them flat on his chest. It was up to him now to keep her from sinking. Or they could drown together. At the moment, she wasn't altogether certain she would care if they did, as long as she first got to savor Mike's intimate embrace.

He shivered at her touch, then bent his head. His lips nibbled on hers, gently at first, then more insistently.

Keeping them both up with one arm on the pool's edge, Mike used his other hand to pull her against him. She let out a soft moan of delight as she felt his arousal. Then he slid his hand down farther, his palm curving over her buttocks to press her even closer. But it wasn't close enough. Without even intending to do it, she opened her legs and circled his hips with them.

He groaned with pleasure as her body pressed more intimately against his. Neither his bathing suit nor hers was of a particularly heavy material and she could feel the hard bulge of his erection between her thighs, almost as if they were naked.

To be naked with Mike, to be making love with him . . . It was what she had wanted for so many weeks now. And they were almost there. Just a couple of fabric barriers to be removed, as well as a logistical problem or two.

She was about to ask him if he'd ever made love in a pool, and if it worked out all right, when he wrenched his mouth away from hers and muttered, "We'd better stop."

Joanne quelled an urge to shriek, "Stop! Have you lost your mind?" and instead said in a quiet tone, "We should?"

He nodded. "One interruption was bad enough." He looked over her shoulder. "But if my neighbor stuck his head over the back fence to say hello, right in the middle of things, I wouldn't like it much."

She glanced uneasily at the wall, as if the neighbor might already be lurking. "I see your point. I wouldn't like it, either."

He pressed a passionate kiss to her mouth, then let go of her and hoisted himself up onto the deck. With water running in streams from his hard, muscular body, he leaned over, offered her his hand and helped her up out of the pool.

He was as strong as he looked, Joanne thought admiringly as he virtually lifted her up onto the decking. Any problems she had standing upright were caused by the fact that his kisses had left her knees unsteady.

She reached for her towel, which she had draped over the back of a lawn chair, but Mike took it out of her hand and gently dried her face and shoulders, even blotting the ends of her hair. Then, using his own towel, he wiped the water from his skin and hair.

Finally putting his towel aside, he turned toward her. He grunted only a little as he picked her up. Joanne was impressed. In books, men were always picking women up and slinging them around, as if they weighed no more than a bag of groceries. But in real life, men rarely hefted weights of a hundred pounds or more with no apparent thought of hernias or slipped disks.

But then, she'd known from the very beginning that Mike Balthazar was something rare.

He settled her in his arms. Joanne happily slipped her arms around his neck, then pressed her face into the hollow of his throat. It flashed through her mind to ask him if he felt all right about this now, if he'd changed his mind about the possibility of a relationship between them. But instinctively she knew that such a question could be suicidal. She had a hunch that nothing fundamental had changed with Mike, that he was only doing this *because* of his body and *despite* his heart and mind....

So, keep it on the physical level, she decided. There, they communicated just fine. And maybe, just maybe, she could use his body's desire for her to influence the other parts of him.

If she couldn't, well, in the meantime, she would have had a whale of a good time....

She angled her head so her mouth was level with his ear. A nice ear, too. Flat and close to the head, with fascinating curves and whorls. She insinuated the tip of her tongue into his ear's center and was gratified to feel the momentary hesitation in his stride and hear his indrawn breath.

She traced the spirals of skin with her tongue as Mike carried her through the kitchen, then up the hall. Outside the first closed door, he paused. Happy to be of help, Joanne reached down to the doorknob and turned it.

"Thanks," Mike said gruffly as he pushed the door open with his foot.

"You're quite welcome," she replied, tickled at hearing herself use the polite phrase under these circumstances.

And then she got a look at the bedroom she hadn't dared peek into earlier. It might have served as an illustration of a master bedroom in a magazine—an old magazine. Apart from a brown and orange bedspread in a contemporary geometric pattern, everything in the room must have been purchased years and years ago.

The dresser was sturdy Grand Rapids, as were the twin nightstands. The headboard of the queen-size bed was a style at least fifteen years out-of-date. The beige draperies at the windows had valences just like ones Joanne remembered having in her den, back when Robbie was a toddler and Jeff a newborn.

Nothing had changed here since Mike's wife's death. In fact, the aura of his married life was so immediate that she was surprised not to see a wedding photo on the bureau.

She thought Mike might have noticed her perusal of the room, but all he said as he deposited her gently on the bed was: "You know, I really didn't expect anything like this to happen tonight. I mean, I didn't plan it or anything."

"I didn't think you did." As she lay back on the bed-spread, she cautioned, "Mike, I'm going to get the spread all wet."

"And I'm going to help," he replied, sitting down on the edge of the bed beside her. "It's really no big deal."

Joanne sighed, feeling more at ease. If he wasn't go-ing to worry about the bedspread, then maybe he wouldn't worry about other things, either. Maybe he could do what she was going to do, which was just re-lax and enjoy the way they were certain to be with each other.

He leaned over, one arm on either side of her, and kissed her hungrily. His skin was cool, his still-wet trunks even cooler against the side of her leg. Joanne herself felt cool and damp from the pool. Only mo-ments into his kiss, however, everything changed; an internal source began pouring enough therms through her body to thaw an Arctic ice floe.

The edge of Mike's thigh pressed against her hip, his corded strength feeling like the steel that shaped the pools he built. His hands on her shoulders were gentle, but she could sense their restrained power. And as he bent lower, the hair on his chest—curling and rough-ening as it dried—caressed her like windblown feath-ers.

He lifted his mouth from hers. "Why in hell do we have so many clothes on?" he complained.

Joanne shrugged, sitting up, preparing to cooper-ate. "Beats me. Some caveman type just picked me up and put me here. I don't remember having had much say in it."

Suddenly grave, he responded, "You do, though. You have everything to say about it. If you don't want to..."

"You bet," she answered fervently.

"I'll remember that," he murmured as he continued rolling her bathing suit down her body.

When it passed her hips, then farther, baring the most private part of her, his gaze fixed on the fiery triangle of hair between her thighs. He smiled with pleasure and delight. "I wondered if it'd be as red as your hair."

His fingers toyed in the soft thatch, teasing and tantalizing for a moment, before he knelt and steadied her as her bathing suit slid to the floor and she stepped out of it.

She was naked and it felt glorious. The only thing wrong was that Mike still wore that scrap of dark brown around his hips. Not that it provided much of a barrier to her imagination. It was obvious that he was fully erect, straining against the lined nylon fabric.

"My turn," she whispered, and reached for the top of his skimpy trunks. He helped her. As soon as the suit was over his hips and down his legs, he stepped out of it without her assistance. Joanne's attention was riveted to the most potent part of his anatomy. He was smooth as ivory and as hard, standing straight out from a dark, soft-looking nest.

"Nice," she observed.

His response was a startled look, as if he'd never been complimented on that part of him before.

But it *was* nice, she thought. Very, very nice indeed. And her fingers ached to touch.

She reached out and circled him with her hand. He gasped, then put his arm around behind her, pulling her hard against him. She was a little disappointed that she wasn't going to have more time to learn the shape and texture of his lower body with her hands. But not *too* disappointed, for the feel of his body pressing against her reignited fires that had been only momentarily banked. Passion shot through her as her breasts flattened against his chest and his erection prodded her belly.

He released her for only a moment, to pull the spread and blankets to the foot of the bed. Then she was back in his embrace, her mouth meeting his. As he kissed her, he eased her down onto the bed again, and the kiss remained unbroken as she stretched out and he half covered her body with his.

It was all delicious. His kiss, his weight on her breasts. And then his fingers touching her knee, caressing upward on her inner leg, then playing with the sultry curls at the apex of her thighs.

She moved her legs slightly apart. His fingertips accepted her invitation, dipping between her folds. From deep within his chest came a hoarse sound of satisfaction and desire as he found her wet and wanting.

But he didn't seem to realize how ready she was for him. He moved his finger deeper into her, then withdrew it, then repeated the process. It was good, but it was nowhere near enough for Joanne. Later, there would be time to explore the more subtle pleasures, after her fierce initial hunger had been slaked.

She lifted her hips against his hand. With her own hand, she reached for him. He groaned as she circled his shaft and slid her hand from the tip all the way to the base, keeping pressure on the underside.

"God . . ." he muttered. "That's *so* good."

The way he said it made her think that he might be slightly surprised that she knew the motion was highly pleasurable for most men. But this was no time for such

discussions. What she wanted was to make the point
that there was no need for further delay.

"Mike," she said insistently.

He seemed to get the message and moved to lever
himself over her. His face was directly above hers when
suddenly she remembered: just one minor little problem.

"Um, Mike . . . protection?" She had thought about
the issue earlier, had even considered purchasing the
means herself, just in case it came to this, but that had
seemed *too* brazen. Surely, in his own home, he'd have
something available.

He gave a slight shake of his head. "Not needed. I've
had a vasectomy. I won't make you pregnant . . . or cause
you any other problems. I promise."

She believed him implicitly. She couldn't resist answering, with a smile, "I won't make you pregnant, either. Or any of the rest of it, for that matter."

He smiled in response. Then his expression changed
to one of rapt attention as he positioned himself between her legs. A probing touch and then, with exquisite unhurriedness, he sheathed himself within her.

Joanne's eyelids lowered, her lips parted. The fit was
as she had known instinctively it would be. Even if it
wasn't true about any other facet of their lives, here,
where body met body, she and Mike Balthazar were
made for each other.

It meant something, she thought. It meant a hell of
a lot. When two people were like adjacent pieces of a
puzzle, matching up like *this* . . . Well, it was just too rare
not to be significant.

And then Mike began to move. Like the shape of his
body, his rhythm was perfect. It was *her* rhythm, but
with an intensity and power that made him the con-

troller, her the responder. Some other time, she thought dimly, she might call the tune, but this time, it was Mike who was in charge, eliciting her body's reactions the same way he directed his work crew.

Yet, she sensed that at every instant he was vividly aware of *her*, so that even though he was in control, he responded, too, increasing his pace when she was ready, but no sooner.

And then her thoughts flew out of her, to be replaced by pure passion that spun tighter and tighter, hotter and hotter, until a moment came when she thought she would scream.

In the next instant, Mike plunged extra-deep within her and her tension shattered in a prolonged paroxysm of pleasure and release.

Mike's own spasms of release followed hers almost immediately. He shuddered and emitted a hoarse cry. Then, rather than collapse upon her, he eased to her side, carefully keeping most of his weight on his arms. He lay face down on the pillow for a moment, chest heaving with his ragged breath. Then he wrapped his arms around her and buried his face in her hair.

She held him as tightly as he held her, still enjoying the tingling aftermath, the sensations fading only gradually. Then she pulled back a little so she could see his face and murmured, "You are one incredible lover, Mike Balthazar."

"So are you." He rolled over onto his back, but kept his side against hers, as if reluctant to break contact completely.

"Thanks." She reached over and smoothed her fingertips down his bare arm, gratified to see that she could make him shiver. "But I'm serious. You're really *something*."

He made a grimace of disbelief. *Real disbelief?* she wondered. Or was he just one of those men who got embarrassed by a compliment?

With the hand farthest from Mike, she surreptitiously crossed her fingers. Oh, how she hoped that she'd have many more chances to tell Mike what an incredible lover he was!

Another thought crossed her mind. A delicate subject. But there were already too many areas where communications between them was blocked or banned. They had to get *some* issues out in the open.

She leaned over and briefly pressed her lips to his bare shoulder. "Can I ask you something?"

"Sure."

"How long have you lived here?"

"In this house? Seventeen years."

"Then this was where you slept. You and your wife, I mean."

"Yeah." He turned his head to look at her, frowning slightly, not angrily, but as if wondering why she wanted to know.

"I noticed . . . you don't have any pictures of her around."

"Yeah, I do, actually."

Joanne frowned. "Really?"

His gaze shifted to the dresser. "Our wedding picture."

Just where she had thought it ought to be—except it still wasn't there. She hadn't imagined its absence before. She gave a little cough. "It must be very small."

Mike let out a strained-sounding chuckle. "It's in the top drawer. I put it there . . . this afternoon."

She sat up, then pulled her legs up and crossed them beneath her, Indian-fashion. "You think she would mind our doing this?"

"Nope." She didn't turn to look at him, but she felt the reassuring touch of his palm on the small of her back. "Mary was sick for a long time before she died. She had plenty of time to think about how things were going to be after she was gone. She knew I wasn't going to become a monk. And she wouldn't have wanted me to. So, no, she wouldn't have minded."

Joanne turned to look at him and caught his sudden grin as he added, "I thought *you* might mind the wedding picture."

"It might have made me feel a little bit uncomfortable," she admitted. Then, belatedly, she registered what he had said a few moments before. Indignantly, she cried, "This *afternoon!* You put the picture away this afternoon? I thought you never expected anything like this to happen tonight."

"I didn't. Not really."

"But then—"

"I wasn't a Boy Scout," he teased. "My folks couldn't afford the uniform. But I always wanted to be."

She pummeled him with mock blows to his chest and arms. He pretended to have to fend her off until, finally, laughing, he said, "Hey! Remember dinner?"

"Dinner?"

"The meal we never ate."

"Oh, yes. I remember something, vaguely—"

She broke off as she saw Mike's look of consternation. "Uh-oh!"

"Uh-oh?" she questioned.

"I bet the coals have gone cold."

They had. And the baked potatoes were shriveled, overcooked lumps. But the steaks broiled up nicely in the oven and with the salad and rolls, there was plenty.

Later, they made love again. Joanne had expected the second time to be slower, more experimental, but the moment he took her in his arms, she was as hungry for him—and he for her—as if they were embracing for the first time.

And the result was the same for her: a shuddering joy that made her feel as if her being had come apart and was being put together again in ways that were entirely new.

Afterward, she might have dozed off for a while. She wasn't sure. And when she glanced over at Mike, his eyes were closed and his breathing had slowed. He wasn't quite asleep—she didn't think—but he was getting close to it. She sighed. She really, really, *really* hated to do this, but she didn't have a choice.

She stroked Mike's bare arm. "Wake up, sleepyhead," she said.

"Mmm?" He opened one eye. His other eyelid flew up as he focused on her face, her naked breasts. He let out a happy-sounding sigh. "Close my eyes for two minutes and I completely forget how incredibly gorgeous you are."

Joanne laughed. "Flattery will get you everywhere. Or would...if you hadn't already *been* everywhere there is to go."

"I'd like to make a reservation for a return trip," he told her. "But only a reservation. I'm not a kid anymore, sorry to say. It's definitely a case of the spirit being willing, but the flesh weak."

"*Weak* is not a word I would have used in reference to you," Joanne said. "And anyway, that wasn't why I asked you to wake up." She made a rueful grimace. "I'm sorry, Mike, but it's after one. I really have to get home." When she saw the look of dismay that crossed his features, she added, "I hate to ask you to get up and get dressed. If this were any other city but L.A., I'd just call a taxi, but you know what it's like trying to get a cab in this town and—"

"A cab? What are you talking about?" He sat up. "Of course, I'll take you home. But I was sort of expecting—hoping, I guess—that you'd stay all night."

Mike was surprised by the depth of his disappointment. He wanted to go to sleep with her warm body cuddled up next to him and when he awoke in the morning, he wanted to find her flaming hair spread out on the pillow beside his head. He wanted it a lot.

Joanne explained ruefully, "I'd like to stay. I really would. But I can't. Robbie's home, remember? If I didn't come home all night, he'd worry." Her eyebrows arched. "Worry! He'd probably *kill* me."

Mike looked at her with astonishment. She had been so free and forward with him, he had assumed that she was fairly experienced. But if her twenty-year-old son would fret at her staying out all night, then obviously she hadn't done anywhere near as much "playing" as he had thought.

"Of course. I wasn't thinking." He swung his legs over the side of the bed, then swiveled his torso around to face her. "I wish like hell you could stay, Joanne, so I can't say I'll be *glad* to take you home. But I don't mind. Really."

But he did mind, even more than he had thought he would. When he parked his car outside her house, then walked her to her door, he wished he could go in with her and spend the night wrapped around her. And as he watched her disappear inside and the heavy door shut behind her, he felt . . . bereft.

8

MIKE OPENED HIS EYES and stared at the plumped-up and smoothed-out pillow next to his. He had been dreaming—nothing deeply or complexly symbolic, just a simple playing out of the wish he had had the night before. In his dream, he had awakened to see the red-gold froth of Joanne's hair haloed by sunlight streaming through the window next to his bed. He had snuggled close to her, wrapping his arms around her, fitting his hips against the curve of her derriere.

Aware of the fullness and pressure in his groin, he sighed. If only his dream were true! The morning was a great time, as far as he was concerned, for making love. He wondered if Joanne felt the same way, or if, like some women, she didn't enjoy sex as much until later in the day. It wasn't a *big* deal if she felt that way about it, he concluded. But it would be nice if she liked it in the morning, too.

He leaned over and focused on the bedside clock. After nine . . . Was it too early to call her?

JOANNE WOKE UP with her arms wrapped around the extra pillow, hugging it to her breasts. As her eyes opened, she thrust it away from her. That was *not* what she wanted to be embracing this morning. What she wanted to embrace was not only much harder, much firmer, much warmer than this, but it moved under its own power. And its name was Mike Balthazar.

She rolled over and glanced at the digital clock radio at her bedside. A little after nine. Was it too early to call him? Probably not. She smiled. She had a hunch he would forgive her, even if she did wake him up.

She picked up the phone and dialed. Busy signal.

She had just hung up the receiver when it rang. Mike? Great minds thinking alike, had he decided to call at the same moment?

But it wasn't Mike. "Brunch is off," Lindsay announced. "I'm really sorry. I hate to cancel at the last minute like this, but the twins have come down with summer colds. They're both feverish and cranky as all get out."

"I'm sorry. Poor little kids."

"They'll recover," Lindsay said. "The point is that Tim and I are both doing full-time mommy-and-daddy duty. I'm afraid our host-and-hostessing skills would be pretty much zero."

"That's okay," Joanne told her. "Don't worry about it."

In fact, she was glad she didn't have to admit that she'd completely forgotten that she and Robbie were supposed to go to the Reynolds' place this morning. She would have remembered in time, she told herself. Unless, of course, making love with Mike Balthazar had completely wiped her memory banks, which seemed not all *that* unlikely.

"Thanks, Joanne," Lindsay said. A male voice in the background muttered something. "Coming, hon," Lindsay called, with the phone muffled.

"I've got to run," she explained to Joanne. "Oh...how was your date with the pool guy last night?"

"My date?" Joanne kept her tone light. "Oh, it was all right."

A baby's wail flared in the background. Lindsay sounded distracted. "Just all right?"

"More than all right," Joanne admitted, unable to be casual any longer. "Linds, I'm in love."

"That's nice," Lindsay said absently. "Okay, Tim. I'll take her."

The phone clicked down. Joanne hung up and counted to ten.

Nothing. She was disappointed. True, Lindsay had other things on her mind, but still . . .

Thirteen. Fourteen. Fifteen.

The phone rang and she picked it up.

Lindsay's voice said accusingly, "You're *what?*"

"You heard me. I'm in love."

"Really? Really and truly in love?"

"What did you do with the crying twin?"

"Told Tim he'd have to hold the fort alone for a few more minutes. It's not every day my best friend informs me that she's in love. In fact, I can't think of the last time those words crossed your lips."

"More than twenty years ago, I'll bet," Joanne said. "And boy, if I'd known then what I know now." She sighed. "But that's all water under the bridge. At least I know *now* what I know now, if you get what I mean."

"Sort of," Lindsay responded. "In principle, at least. So, are you *really* in love?"

"Well . . ." Joanne caught her lower lip with her teeth. "It's too soon to be absolutely certain, I guess. But it sure feels like love." She knew she didn't have to be more specific than that. Quite recently, Lindsay herself had gone through the difficulties and uncertainties of falling in love. She would know exactly what Joanne was talking about.

"Wow! That's terrific!" her friend exclaimed warmly.

"Maybe..." Joanne acknowledged. "Well, I agree it's terrific to find out that I can really feel this way again. But there's definitely a bad side to this."

"Oh? What's that?"

"I have no idea how Mike feels about me." And that was a little bit of a lie, she realized. She knew more than she was telling. But all of what she knew was depressing. Unless, she thought, brightening, last night had changed his mind about their being wrong for each other.

She could always hope....

MIKE FROWNED at the phone. The busy signal. Again. Did she wake up and immediately start phoning everybody she knew? Not quite *everybody*, he amended. She hadn't phoned him. And he really wanted to hear her voice.

He hung up the phone, waited a few seconds, then redialed her number, just in case he might have hit a wrong button the first time. Again, the busy signal. He might as well shower.

He was rinsing off soapy lather when he heard the phone ring. Leaving the water running, he stepped out and dripped into the bedroom.

"Hello?" he said, half convinced, just by the force of wanting it to be so, that it would be Joanne.

But the voice was Bill's.

"Listen, have Kitty and I got a deal for you!" Bill sounded overly hearty, like a used-car salesman trying to sell a reluctant customer on a known lemon.

"Oh?"

"We're going to take you out to brunch! On us. Our treat."

Mike regarded the phone warily. This was not part of the pattern of his relationship with Kitty and Bill. Dinners at his house, yes. But not meals paid for by the younger couple. And then he got it—the invitation was meant to be an apology for their barging in last night.

"Sounds good to me," he said.

"Boy, Gary can really cook!" Robbie spooned up a second helping of scrambled eggs laced with cheese.

"He cooks a little *too* well, in my opinion," Joanne commented. Her new housekeeper's skills made it too tempting for her to overeat. Of course, a little more of the kind of exercise she'd gotten last night and she wouldn't have to worry half so much, she reflected wryly.

Joanne and Robbie were eating breakfast at the glass-topped table near the wall of windows that looked out onto the half-finished pool. The phone sitting on the nearby wicker table rang.

Mike?

Joanne jumped for it, then a moment later disappointedly handed the receiver to her son.

She went on eating as Robbie conversed with a friend finishing with "Yeah, I think it'll be okay. *Pretty* sure it'll be okay. I'll call you back."

"What'll be okay?" Joanne asked curiously after Robbie had handed her the receiver to replace on the cradle.

Robbie grinned the endearing dimpled grin that meant he wanted something. "Okay with you if I take a few days and drive up the coast with Bart?" Bart was Robbie's college roommate—a good kid, in Joanne's opinion. "He wants to go visit his girlfriend up there, but he wants some company for the trip." Robbie picked up his fork and dug into his eggs. "I know I've only been here a couple of days, but I'll be back by Thursday. Friday at the latest."

He wasn't exactly *asking* her, Joanne noticed. Which was as it should be. He was too grown-up now to ask permission for a trip like this one. She regarded him fondly. Normally, she wouldn't have liked him interrupting what was already only a brief visit. But, right now, with the relationship between her and Mike so new, so precarious, she was just as glad to see one complicating factor eliminated.

"Sure," she said. "Go ahead, kiddo. Have a good time."

EVERY TABLE AND BOOTH of the pancake restaurant was filled. It looked as if most of Southern California had planned to go out this week for a Sunday treat.

Across from Mike, Kitty and Bill sat close together, not quite touching, but obviously a unit. Not once during the meal had Kitty told her husband what to do; not once had Bill whined or apologized to his wife.

And so far, no one, neither Mike nor either half of the younger couple, had made even the slightest, most oblique reference to what had happened the night before.

Maybe that was best, Mike decided, shoving his syrup-smeared plate a few inches away from him. Some things were better left undiscussed. He drained the last of his coffee, then set his cup down in the saucer.

He glanced at his watch. Nearly one o'clock. Maybe he'd try to call Joanne from the pay phone outside.

He smiled at his son and daughter-in-law. "Well, this has been great," he told them as he slid toward the side of the booth.

Bill had already made an ostentatious show of grabbing the check. Now the younger man's face fell. "You're not leaving already!"

"We're done, aren't we?"

"Well, yes, but—"

Kitty's thin, sharp voice interrupted. "We want to talk to you, Dad."

And they had had a whole meal's worth of chances, Mike reflected. But one look at their intent faces made him give up the idea of being able to call Joanne for a while yet. He settled back into the booth, signaled the waiter and asked for more coffee, then faced the younger pair. "Okay, what's up?"

Kitty looked meaningfully at Bill, her gaze an obvious goad.

Bill cleared his throat. "Uh . . . we only say this because we love you, Dad. But we think you're making a big mistake."

Mike frowned. "About what?"

"About this Mrs. Stephenson," said his son.

TWENTY MINUTES LATER, Mike left the restaurant. For the first time in years, he felt seriously in the wrong. With his own kid, his own family. And it was his own damn fault.

All Kitty and Bill had done was remind him of things he already knew—that he and Joanne Stephenson came from two different worlds, that they had virtually nothing in common, that she would never fit in with Mike's friends or he with hers, that her money was bound to skew the relationship.

Mike hadn't had a leg to stand on in the discussion. Simply from Joanne's address, Kitty and Bill had been able to accurately guess her *high* economic status. The amount of money she had available to spend on a pool told them even more. When questioned, Mike hadn't been able to deny any of the pair's suppositions. Joanne *was* rich. Old Money. Upper-class. Harsh indictments—every one of them.

Unfortunately, the ensuing lecture about the wisdom of sticking to one's own kind was practically verbatim the one Mike had delivered to Bill when he was a teenager.

All the couple said were things Mike already knew were true.

Which he had conveniently managed to forget.

He didn't try to telephone Joanne from the pay phone outside the restaurant. He just went home.

FIVE MINUTES AFTER he entered the house, his phone rang. He was in the bedroom, changing clothes and trying not to notice that the bedding still exuded the musky, heady aroma of sex.

He picked up the phone on the nightstand.

"Hi," Joanne's voice said brightly. "How are you?"

"Uh . . . fine." Not fine. He was trying to figure out how to tell her that he'd made a big mistake, that he should have stuck to his guns and not let her physical appeal obliterate his common sense.

"I tried to call you earlier this morning," she told him.

"I tried to call you, too."

"But I got the busy signal."

"So did I."

"I bet we were trying to call each other at the same time." She laughed. "We do seem to be pretty well in synch when it comes to timing."

"I'll say," Mike blurted before recalling that instead of remembering how it had felt to join with her in the

rhythm of passion and fulfillment, he was *supposed* to
be figuring out how to tell her he couldn't see her again.

"Mike?"

"Uh-huh?"

"I wanted to ask you a favor. Gary's been complaining that he hasn't gotten to show off his culinary skills
for company. I wondered if you'd be willing to come
over tonight so he can demonstrate."

"Dinner? At your place?" Mike considered for only
a split second. It would be much fairer of him to tell her
in person, rather than over the phone, that he couldn't
keep on seeing her. And with her son there, nothing
could happen anyway. There wouldn't be any danger
of his desire for her running away with his common
sense. "That sounds fine," he agreed. "What time?"

MIKE RANG THE DOORBELL. In one hand he held a manila envelope. From the filing cabinet at the office, he
had dug out information on apprenticeship programs
sponsored by the various trade unions. He'd put it all
together in a package for Robbie. It was the least he
could do for Joanne's kid and by extension, for Joanne
herself. He hoped it would make up—at least a little
bit—for what he was going to have to say to her tonight.

The door opened. Mike's eyes widened. Joanne wore
the same lime-green sundress she had worn the evening she'd signed the contract. Not only did the dress's
strapless elasticized top leave her upper chest and
shoulders bare, but its ruffle-trimmed full skirt beautifully accentuated her tiny waist and rounded hips.

She smiled up at him, her blue eyes alight. Her lips
were parted softly, as if she might welcome his kiss. He
forced himself not to lean over and press his mouth to

hers. Instead, as he stepped inside he held the manila envelope out stiffly in front of him. "I brought some information for Robbie."

If she was dismayed that he wasn't more affectionate, she didn't show it. "Why, thank you, Mike. That was really nice of you." She took the envelope from him. "I'll make sure he gets this when he gets back from his trip."

"Trip?"

"Yes. He's driving up the coast with a friend for a couple of days."

Mike's jaw tightened. With her son not here, there was no real reason he couldn't make love to her.

Except that he couldn't. Just couldn't. Instead, he had to tell her he couldn't see her anymore.

Joanne's eyes narrowed as Mike stepped past her. There was something different about him today. What was it? He wasn't quite looking at her; that was it. And with Mike, that meant something must be dreadfully wrong.

Had he reverted to being the old Mike Balthazar who couldn't possibly have sex without a relationship and certainly couldn't have a relationship with *her*?

Her horrible hunch was confirmed an instant later as he turned to face her, his expression grim. "Joanne, I have to talk to you."

She didn't know exactly what he was going to say, but she was absolutely certain that it was something she didn't want to hear. And she was certain that she needed time to put together a defense.

She grabbed his arm and gave him an inanely cheerful smile. "Why, sure, Mike. There'll be plenty of time to talk over dinner. But right now, I think we'd better go sit down. Gary's awfully fussy about serving meals right on time, you know." She rolled her eyes. "So temperamental, that boy. But worth it. He can really cook. Quite the chef, in fact."

Keeping up a nonstop stream of chatter, she dragged Mike down the hall to the formal dining room. She had decided that tonight, she and Mike might as well dine there.

She left him seated at the heavy, dark, Spanish-style table, then darted into the kitchen, where she found Gary bent over, peering through the glass door of the oven.

"Serve something and serve it now," she told him, muting her voice so it wouldn't carry back to the dining room.

He turned, frowning. His shock of blond hair was limp from the heat of the stove. "What do you mean, serve something? I thought you two were going to have drinks first. I hadn't planned to serve the gazpacho for half an hour yet. It may not be quite chilled enough."

"I don't care. Serve it anyway," Joanne said. "Or bring on the salad. Or the main course. Anything."

"Well, if you insist, but—"

"Just do it, okay? And make sure there's lots of wine uncorked."

Gary's eyebrows lifted. "Trying to get the man drunk?"

"Maybe," Joanne admitted shamelessly. "And one more thing, Gary. I want you popping into the dining room a lot. Every couple of minutes, without fail."

"But—" his brows drew together over his nose "—I don't get it. Just a little while ago, didn't you say that you wanted an intimate, romantic dinner, with as few interruptions as possible?"

"That's what I said, all right," Joanne confirmed crisply. "But I've changed my mind, okay? Pop. And pop often."

"MORE WINE?" Joanne inquired with a feline smile.

Mike shook his head. It seemed to him she'd spent the entire meal filling up his glass. They had begun with a Burgundy. Then, somewhere between the cold soup and the entrée, a new bottle had appeared on the table. Announcing that it was something special, she had insisted that he absolutely *had* to try it. And then a third bottle—a dessert wine—had arrived with the chocolate-raspberry soufflé, and she had insisted on him sampling that, too.

It was a good thing he had a high tolerance for alcohol. The only effect so far was that he was starting to feel really relaxed.

And he was also having a little trouble remembering exactly what it was that he had to say to Joanne this evening.

He groped for it....

Got it. The two of them had absolutely nothing in common, no hope of a relationship lasting, and so they ought to end it *now*.

So far, his opportunities to tell her anything serious or private had been somewhere between limited and nil. Though a fine cook, Gary had a lot to learn about serving people at dinner. The kid was in the room about every two seconds, so Mike had finally given up even trying to say anything important to Joanne.

The swinging door flapped open and there was Gary again, carrying a coffeepot and yet another bottle.

Joanne smiled up at him. "Thanks, Gary," she said warmly. "You've done a beautiful job. And it really is okay for you to leave now."

"Leave?" the young man questioned.

"Yes, *leave*," Joanne repeated with emphasis. "It's quite all right with me if you go out for the evening. You can take care of the dishes in the morning."

"Ah, yes . . . leave," Gary echoed. "As in departing the premises." He cocked one eyebrow. "I imagine you won't have any objections if I don't get back until quite late."

"*Very* late," Joanne emphasized. "I mean, it's fine with me. As late as you want." She turned to Mike. "He's leaving," she announced as Gary poured coffee into Mike's cup, adding a slug of cognac before Mike could protest. "And we don't want to sit here with all these dirty dishes on the table. Let's take our coffee to the living room."

Moments later, Mike found himself seated on the long oyster-colored couch, with Joanne sitting close beside him. He wasn't entirely sure how *that* had happened. It had been in his mind to park himself some distance away from her—the next block would have been a safe distance. But there she was, inches away.

It was a big problem. The glow from the lamp illuminated her hair. Her eyes, big and blue, seemed to peer directly into his soul. Now his hands and his body remembered how incredibly wonderful it had been the night before to touch her curves and hollows, to feel her satiny softness, to blend himself with her in passion.

Just thinking about it made him aware of an increasing tension in his groin. How much better it would be, rather than to deliver his goodbye speech, to simply gather her in his arms, carry her upstairs and make love to her.

He leaned forward, picked up his cup from the low table and took a deep swallow of coffee, only remembering the cognac Gary had added when it seared his throat.

Then he felt another source of warmth—Joanne's hand on his knee.

Joanne didn't feel altogether at ease about what she was about to do—deliberately seduce Mike Balthazar. Nor did she feel terrific about the ploys she had already used this evening. She had never been a game player, but this time, she figured she was playing for her life—for the possibility that he would come to love her, to care about her; for *their* future.

Mike set his cup down. "Joanne," he began.

"Uh-huh." Her hand moved higher, her fingertips pressing lightly into his thigh.

"We need to talk."

"Go right ahead," she said politely.

Her hand moved farther up his thigh.

Mike swallowed. His mouth was dry and his thoughts jumbled up, none having any significance whatsoever—compared to the heat of her hand. "I can't think when you're doing that," he complained.

"I'm sorry." She sounded genuinely contrite—but she didn't take her hand away. "Just what was it you wanted to talk about, Mike?"

He turned to look at her. The top of her sundress seemed to have slid lower on her body. The upper halves of her breasts, milky white and smooth, were visible.

"About us . . ." he answered hoarsely.

"Nice subject," she said.

Her hand went higher still, her fingertips trailing over the general region of his zipper. A groan of pleasure came from deep in Mike's chest. She leaned toward him. The tip of one breast grazed his arm. The dress had slipped a little lower still. The ruffly part barely covered her nipples.

"Joanne, please," he grunted.

"Happy to oblige," she murmured. Seeming to interpret his words as a plea for more, rather than less, she reached for his belt buckle.

His own hands somehow moved to her breasts, testing the glorious weight of them in his palms, then slipped down inside her dress so he could tease her nipples with his thumbs.

He pulled in a long, tortured breath and forced himself to continue with what he had been going to say. "It's not right for us to be together. Kitty and Bill reminded me this afternoon. . . ."

Joanne carefully concealed her sudden understanding. For an instant, she was tempted to consider the younger couple the *enemy*. But they weren't—not really, she reflected. Mike himself—or the part of Mike that could see only that she had been born with money and he without—was the real enemy.

"Uh-huh," she said, as if she could have cared less. And in fact, alarming as this conversation was, her attention was diverted as she released Mike's belt buckle, then tugged the tab of his zipper down. His mind might not agree, but his body sure wanted her, she thought. With his fly open, she could see clearly that he was already fully erect and straining against his navy blue briefs. She flicked her tongue over dry lips.

"They reminded you . . ." she prodded.

"Uh . . ." His breathing quickened as she pressed her palm against his arousal.

What the hell *had* they reminded him? Mike wondered. Oh, yeah. Now he had it. "Joanne, listen," he muttered huskily.

"I'm listening."

He meant to speak, but she had found the placket in his briefs and was insinuating her hand into the opening. He might have asked her to stop, except that he wasn't any better than she. He couldn't resist just one quick kiss. He bent his head, slanting his mouth over hers. Her lips were parted and moist. He slipped his tongue between them and she moaned as she welcomed him.

Her hand was on his erection, circling and caressing. And his hands were on her breasts, teasing the tips into hardness. In fact, her dress was all the way down around her waist, he realized.

He pulled his mouth from hers. "Us . . ." he reiterated.

"Uh-huh?"

"It can't work."

"I'm sure you're right," she said amiably. Her hair curtained her face as she bent toward his lap.

"I mean, we're from two different worlds. We have nothing in common—Oh, God!"

Her lips had surrounded the tip of his fully aroused shaft. With her tongue, she wet the head, licking as if she liked the flavor.

He put his hand on the nape of her neck. His voice was a rasp from deep in his chest. "You don't have to do that."

She took her mouth from him for only a moment, tilting her head so she could look up into his face. "Don't *have* to? I want to, Mike. I love doing this."

A spark of surprise lit in his eyes. "Really? I didn't think women—"

"Not all women are alike," she said firmly, not wanting to imply criticism of any females in Mike's past. And besides, it didn't matter what a woman or women in his previous experience might or might not have done, might or might not have enjoyed. She loved pleasing Mike in this way and, even if the idiot insisted on resuming his little speech of renunciation later on, she intended to enjoy herself while she could.

After *that*, it wasn't at all difficult to get Mike to remove his trousers and briefs. As soon as those impediments were out of the way, Joanne returned to her task. She wet him fully, then surrounded him with her lips and hand, experimenting until she found the movement and pressure that elicited from him the deepest, most wrenching moans of satisfaction.

As she continued caressing, touching, tasting, his breathing grew increasingly ragged, the hard muscles in his belly rippled, and the cords in his neck strained. Suddenly he cried, "Stop!" and, placing a hand on either side of her head, lifted her away from him.

She looked up to find his eyes half blind with passion. "Why did you stop me?" she asked, aggrieved.

"Because, incredible as that was, I want something even better. I want to be inside you."

She couldn't complain one bit about that. "Well, all right. If you insist."

He focused on her, registering with an expression of dismay her relatively fully clothed state. Her dress was down around her waist, but it was still more or less on. "I've been neglecting you," he said contritely.

Joanne's face wore a vixenish smile. "You're crazy. I've been having a perfectly marvelous time."

She stood, the better to facilitate undressing. Meaning to help, Mike put his hand on her knee and slid it up the inside of her thigh. Reaching the top, he discovered with a swiftly indrawn breath what Joanne herself already knew: she was dripping with excitement.

With hands that shook slightly, he helped her peel her panties down her legs. Stepping out of the dress was easy, the work of a second. And then, before he could move from where he sat, she poised over his lap, arranging one leg on either side of him. For a moment, she savored the feel of his erect tip at her opening. His hands were on her waist, steadying her, supporting her.

And then she let herself slide down, her heat and moisture surrounding him. He thrust upward at the same moment and there it was again—that fit, that incredible conjunction of parts, as if the two of them had been crafted from reverse images of the same original mold.

Their hips moved in perfect unison, Mike lifting as Joanne sank, so he went deeper inside her than she had ever imagined possible. She wrapped her arms around his neck and kissed him as she moved on him. He had his hands on her body, caressing her breasts, her back, her buttocks.

They moved. With all the preparation she had given him, it wasn't long before Mike's entire body convulsed. The feeling of his hot gush spilling into her threw Joanne over the edge into an explosive pleasure that was cataclysmic. Glorious.

As the fine tremors of release dissipated, lessening in intensity, she clung to Mike with her face buried in his neck.

His voice was a deep growl in her ear. "You are really something. Absolutely amazing!"

"You, too."

He put his hand on the back of her head, holding her against him, neither looking at her face nor letting her look into his as he cleared his throat, then said, "Joanne... You do understand what I was trying to say before?"

"Sure."

Did she? Mike considered. Joanne Stephenson was *not* the woman for him, not on a long-term basis. But she didn't seem to expect anything long-term from him. Obviously she regarded this as nothing more than a pleasant interlude, a purely physical encounter.

It wasn't even a relationship. Not really. And that being the case, he didn't have to end it, after all—thank God!

Double-checking, he went on, "Then we're agreed that it's just sort of a . . . a thing we're having. That it can't possibly last?"

"Oh, absolutely," Joanne said. She had her crossed fingers hidden behind Mike's head where he couldn't see them.

"And it doesn't really *mean* anything," Mike added.

"Not a thing," Joanne agreed, blithely prevaricating. "It's just sex, probably. I'm sure it'll be over before we know it."

9

THE DOOR TO HIS OFFICE opened. Mike looked up from
the permit application he was filling out. Bill came in,
wiping the sweat from his brow. The summer heat had
continued unabated and Mike had had Bill keeping tabs
on a couple of remodeling jobs under way.

"How's it going?" he asked his son. He had been
making an effort not to quiz Bill about small details, but
that didn't mean that Mike didn't expect running re-
ports from him.

Bill told him about the jobs he had visited that day,
then asked awkwardly, "So, how's it going with Mrs.
Stephenson's pool?"

"All right."

Bill cleared his throat. "Uh . . . has she been around
much while the work's going on?"

"Not much. She's a pretty busy woman."

"Then you haven't seen her for a while?"

"Not for a long time," Mike answered. Not since that
very morning, when he had left her bed. Well, it *seemed*
like a long time, he rationalized to himself. And besides, it was really none of Bill's business. What difference did it make if his son thought he wasn't seeing
Joanne anymore? Sooner or later, it was bound to be
true.

He looked down at his desk and seized upon an estimate lying there as an excellent excuse to change the

subject. "This estimate you did," he began, picking it up.

Bill tensed visibly, a new bead of sweat forming on his upper lip. "Yeah?"

Mike smiled reassuringly. "You did a good job, son. Every bit as good as I could have done myself."

MOONLIGHT STREAMED through the open window. Mike and Joanne had made love some time before, but neither had felt drowsy. They had been chatting about this and that, including the new pool.

Joanne flipped onto her side and, with one elbow bent, propped her head up on her hand. "You're absolutely certain it'll be done by weekend after next?"

Mike had warned her there would be some delays. And he had been absolutely right. It was now nearly four weeks since work had begun—three and a half since Mike had become her lover.

The best three and a half weeks of her life, Joanne reflected. In one respect, she wouldn't mind a bit if they just went on this way forever—even if that meant Mike's continuing to deny their rightness for each other.

He hadn't made any speeches lately about how ill-suited they were; nor had he announced that he'd changed his mind.

Maybe he *had* changed his mind, she hoped. Though it didn't seem too likely, she really wished it were so. She was eager for a deepening of their relationship—for Mike to be more a part of her life and she of his.

Mike turned toward her. With his fingertips, he lazily traced a sinuous line down her arm. "Barring an act of God, it'll be done, filled and ready to swim in by weekend after next," he said. "Fact, it ought to be ready *this* weekend, so the extra week is all safety margin. Why?"

"Oh, I was thinking of inviting some of my friends over. I haven't really had an open house since I moved in and—" She broke off as she noticed the expression on his face. She swatted him lightly on the arm. "My *friends*, Mike. Not Alison Colfax and George Bentinger and that crowd. Well, only the nice ones from that crowd, anyway. So, what do you think about weekend after next, Sunday afternoon? Is that okay for you?"

"For me? What have I got to do with it?"

She gazed at him, astonished. "I want you to come, Mike. You're . . . you're practically the guest of honor. I mean, you built the pool, after all." And although it wasn't completed yet, she could already tell that it was going to be every bit as lovely as his watercolor had promised. But that had nothing to do with the real reason why she wanted him at her party. She wanted him there because he was the man in her life, and it was time her friends got to know him.

"I don't think so," he said.

Dismayed, she looked at him. She had become very familiar with that stubborn Mike Balthazar look. His face turned granitelike, as if he were suitable for immediate transplantation to Mount Rushmore.

She deliberately kept her tone light. "Well, okay. If Sunday isn't good for you, we can make it Saturday. Or the following week. It doesn't matter all that much."

"No!"

Joanne sighed. "I told you, Mike. It won't be those awful people you met at Alison's. This doesn't have anything to do with charity. This is just for fun—so it'll be my friends. My real friends. You'll like them. Honestly."

Mike was skeptical about that. But it wasn't the point, anyway. "I'm sure I would," he lied. "If I met them. But I really think it's better if I don't."

"Why, Mike? I don't get it."

He rolled over onto his back and stared at the ceiling. It seemed so obvious to him. Why was it so hard for her to understand? "Because meeting them would just complicate things for you—later."

Later... Joanne swallowed. He meant when it ended. When they stopped seeing each other. Well, *that* answered her question. She felt a stab of pain in her stomach. He hadn't changed his mind—not one single iota.

"All right," she agreed. "I wasn't thinking."

She turned onto her back. Last time they had come close to this topic, she had evaded it with sex. This time she needed to explore, to learn more about Mike and the real reason for his conviction that the two of them were ill-matched.

She drew a deep breath. "I realize that this thing—us—can't possibly last. But frankly, Mike, I sometimes forget why."

Frowning, he turned toward her.

"The specific reasons, I mean," she said hastily.

"We come from two different worlds," he declared.

"Yes?" she prompted. "Go on."

He looked at her, perplexity on his face. "It's obvious, isn't it?"

She shrugged a bare shoulder. "Maybe not obvious enough, because I'm not entirely sure what you mean by 'two different worlds.'"

"You like champagne and fancy dinner parties, I'm a beer-and-bowling kind of guy."

That was it in a nutshell, as far as Mike was concerned—the difference in their backgrounds and lifestyles. Well, there was *one* other issue—the power conferred by her money. The power that would, were they a permanent couple, have made him as much the whining underdog as Bill was with Kitty.

But there was no need to even get into that one, he reflected. Not when there was so much else that formed a barrier between them.

"Beer versus champagne," Joanne said slowly. "But Mike, the one time I offered you champagne, you lapped it right up. And who says I don't like beer? And bowling, for that matter? I haven't bowled in ages, but I used to love it."

"I didn't necessarily mean that literally."

"Oh," she said, deliberately pretending to be obtuse. "It was a metaphor. I get it." She turned her head to look at him. "What was it a metaphor *for*, Mike? I'm curious. I mean, what are the things we *really* don't have in common, if it's not champagne and beer and bowling and things like that?"

"C'mon, Joanne. Just look at the way you live and the way I live."

She shook her head stubbornly. "Not specific enough."

"How's this for specific?" He lifted his arm and made a sweeping gesture that encompassed the spacious bedroom. The beehive fireplace in the corner was cold and dark now, but he could imagine how nice it would be in winter, making love with a fire crackling in the hearth. Not that there was much chance of their lasting that long. "Your house must be three or four times the size of mine."

"But you don't exactly live in a hovel," she pointed out. "And besides, are you saying you hate being here?"

"No . . ." Mike admitted slowly. He would have thought he might feel intimidated in her much larger, much more luxurious home, but it was so open and comfortable that he was perfectly at ease. Nor did she seem to mind spending time at his house. In fact, she often suggested meeting there because—as she put it— he had a pool with water in it, rather than one that was still only a hole in the ground.

"I didn't think so," she said. "And I like your place just fine. So what's the problem there?"

Why did he feel, all of a sudden, as if he were grasping at straws, defending something that was inherently indefensible? He *could* point out that she didn't even have to work for a living; but he had learned that she *did* work, that she took her obligations to charity as seriously as most people did a full-time job.

There had to be something else. And there was. He found it almost at once.

"Look how much traveling you've done," he argued. "You've gone all over the world. Europe. Asia. The farthest I've ever been is to a Mexican border town."

Joanne sneaked a look at him. He wore a "So there" expression on his face. "Do you *want* to travel?" she asked.

"Sure! Who doesn't?"

"Where would you like to go?"

"I don't know. I hadn't thought about it. Europe, I guess."

"Then why don't you? More to the point, why haven't you already gone, if it's something you want to do?"

He stared as her as if she'd lost her mind.

"Don't tell me you can't afford it," she challenged. "The way you work, all the projects you've mentioned since I've known you, you've got to be making decent money." He started to speak, but she silenced him with a finger across his lips. "And you told me you'd lived in your house for what? Getting close to twenty years, wasn't it? The mortgage must be pretty low."

"Actually, it's paid off," he revealed with a trace of pride. "But—"

"But me no buts!" Joanne said indignantly. She might let Warren Frostine manage her money for her, but that didn't mean she was ignorant of the economic facts of life. "If it's paid off, then you've got to be making more than you spend. Why don't you use some of it for things you want to do? Now, if you don't *want* to go to Europe, that's another thing. There's no law that says you have to. But if it's just because you think you can't afford it . . ."

"I *can't* afford it," Mike said defensively.

"Why?" Suddenly Joanne's face crumpled with contrition. "Oh, Mike, I'm so sorry. I didn't even think. Your wife . . . She must have had huge medical expenses before she died. I shouldn't have—"

"No." He interrupted with a brief shake of his head. "There were costs, but she was insured."

Joanne fell silent. Even though she hadn't been in the wrong, as she'd feared, she'd made a tactical error; she had been on the attack. Now, abruptly, she had been thrown back into a defensive position.

She drew a deep breath and pressed on, regardless. She needed desperately to understand how Mike Balthazar's mind worked. "You've worked hard, you're making money. Why can't you afford to spend some on something you want to do?"

He thrust his fingers through his hair in a gesture of frustration. "You just don't get it, do you?"

"Nope," she said lightly. "And you can call me obtuse if you want, but I *won't* get it unless you explain it to me."

In his voice was an undertone of patience, as if he were speaking to a rather backward child. "A person like you doesn't need to worry about security. But a guy like me needs to have something put by for an emergency. You never know what's going to happen."

Joanne had a hunch she was finally getting to the nitty-gritty, to an essential cog that made Mike Balthazar tick. "For instance?"

"The business could go bust," he said. "Or I might get sick and be unable to work. Or Kitty and Bill might need money or..." He shrugged. "A lot of things could happen."

"True. But things could happen to me, too, Mike. The country could have a huge economic disaster and I could lose everything."

He snorted dismissively.

"It doesn't seem likely to me, either," she acknowledged. "But I know people who worry about it a lot. Just like you worry about the things you mentioned. But that doesn't mean that they *never* spend any money on something they want. A trip to Europe, for instance."

He turned away from her. Silent, he swung his legs over the side of the bed. She wished desperately that she could see his face as he said in a stark, unrevealing voice, "You don't understand. How could you? You've never gone hungry because there's no money in the house for food."

Joanne went very still. Here she was, at the core of the problem. At last. "When did you go hungry, Mike?"

He rested his elbows on his knees and stared into the darkness in the corner of the room. "Never mind. It's not important."

She eased over closer to him and tentatively put her hand on his shoulder. "Then, if it's not important, just satisfy my curiosity. When did you go hungry?"

"When?" His tone was elaborately indifferent. "Lots of different times. Every time my father would lose his job." He still wasn't looking at her. "He was a loser, okay, Joanne? He couldn't hold a job. Either he'd have trouble with the foreman and get fired, or he'd make some damn fool mistake and get fired. He didn't drink—not much, anyway, except when he was between jobs. He was just a . . . a jerk."

She heard his anguish. Her family hadn't had the cozy closeness she might have wished for, but she had loved and respected her parents. She could imagine how painful it must be to regard your own father as a "jerk." And there was more; she could see it in the tension in the muscles of Mike's back.

"He was such a jerk—" Mike spat the word out "—that when he *was* making money, he'd spend it. On fancy food and clothes for my mother and all kinds of things. He never seemed to realize that he might get fired again and then we'd need a nest egg, just to keep from going to bed hungry at night."

"I'm sorry, Mike."

"I don't want pity," he warned her.

"It's not!" she insisted. "Well, if it is, it's not for *you*—not the grown-up you. But can't I feel sorry for the kid who went to bed with his belly aching?"

"My mom's must have ached worse than mine," he said bitterly. "When times were bad, she always gave me whatever there was to eat."

She guessed they must have been too proud for welfare. Before she had a chance to ask, Mike rose and turned to face her.

Stark-naked, moonlight striping him with silver, he lost none of his dignity. "As soon as I was old enough, I started working—after school, weekends, as much as I possibly could. Then it was better. We didn't have to count on my father for everything anymore."

Maybe he *was* right, she reflected, shaken. Maybe the gulf between them *was* too wide. Maybe his resentment of the rich would prevent them from meeting as man and woman, loving and loved. As partners....

But she couldn't give up. Not yet.

At least they had drawn closer in one respect. They had each talked about their marriages. Joanne had confessed how disturbing it had been for her when Doug left her for a younger woman—which subsequently became a *string* of younger women.

From Mike's talk of his dead wife, Joanne had deduced that the marriage had been solid, though perhaps not the joyously intimate partnership she believed was possible for a man and a woman. The important thing was that she and Mike had confided truths and understood each other.

Maybe they could come to a rapprochement over the money issue, too. Maybe in time, Mike would come to see that he didn't have to be afraid of poverty anymore. And once he lost his fear, maybe his resentment of her wealth would vanish.

"Your parents," Joanne questioned. "Are they still alive?"

He shook his head. "No. But at least my mother had some security her last few years." He looked down at her, his gaze penetrating. "Okay, that's the story of my life. Now, do you see what I mean when I say we come from two different worlds?"

What she saw was that he had admitted things to her that were difficult for him and consequently, they were one step closer to intimacy. To push for more tonight would be a mistake.

"Yep, sure do," she replied agreeably. Then, in a blatant change of subject, she burst out, "Say, Mike! I'm hungry! Let's go see if Gary left any yummy leftovers in the refrigerator."

JOANNE BOUNCED ONE of the Reynolds' twins on her knee. Clay, the boy twin, gurgled happily and spat on Joanne's blouse. She smiled. "Gee, I never thought I'd enjoy being spit on," she said to Lindsay, who was diapering the other twin. "But it's been so long, it makes me feel kinda nostalgic. It's sure fun playing with yours. I've decided I'm going to make a terrific grandmother. When Jeff and Robbie get around to making me one, I mean."

At the moment, she didn't feel especially grandmotherly; she felt deliciously wanton. Mike had spent the night before in her bed and this morning had awakened her with some of the most shamelessly hedonistic lovemaking she had ever experienced.

Joanne realized her smug smile must have revealed the train of her thoughts when Lindsay laughed, then asked, "So how *is* it going with Mike?"

Joanne sighed. "In some ways, couldn't be better. But in others, not so great."

Lindsay powdered her daughter's bottom as Joanne continued to talk about Mike.

"He has this whole script in his head," Joanne explained. "And believe me, he's absolutely convinced that that's the way it's going to be." She told Lindsay a little more about Mike's past.

When she had finished she said, "It just occurred to me.... One thing that might help is if he realizes that he does have things in common with some of my friends."

Lindsay picked little Katie up off the change table and put her in the playpen. "Us, for instance?" she suggested.

"If you don't mind."

"Mind? I'd *like* to meet Mike. So would Tim. I've been telling you for weeks that we'd like to meet him."

"Unfortunately, if that's going to happen, I'm afraid we're going to have to ambush him," Joanne said.

"What do you mean?"

"You and Tim are going to have pretend you just dropped in on the spur of the moment."

It took her several minutes to convince Lindsay that this was the only way to arrange a meeting. Clay was getting restless, so Joanne got up and put him in the playpen with his sister. She glanced at her watch. "I guess I'd better go. I've got a meeting with Warren."

"How is Warren?"

Joanne wrinkled her nose. "Warren is Warren. Now that I've stopped going to those awful charity parties,

Warren is squiring around this gorgeous blonde. She's about thirty, max. Everybody's convinced he dumped me for her." She laughed. "And you know what? I don't mind a bit. If that's what Warren wants people to think, it's quite all right with me. So we're set for Sunday?"

Lindsay nodded. "I'll have to check with Tim, but I'm sure once I explain, he'll play along."

Joanne hesitated near the nursery door. "One more thing, Linds. So far, Mike hasn't met any friends of mine since that disastrous dinner and dance."

"Oh," Lindsay said meaningfully.

"'Oh' is right," Joanne confirmed. "So, when you and Tim come over, could you please act really normal?"

Lindsay let out a burst of laughter. "*Act* normal? I beg your pardon?"

Joanne gave an airy wave of her hand. "Well, you know what I mean."

"IT'S REALLY DONE?" Joanne had just gotten home from a committee meeting to find Mike waiting for her. "Officially, completely and absolutely done?"

Three days earlier, they had begun to fill the pool with water. Then, this morning, the diving board and rails had gone in.

"Sort of," Mike equivocated, explaining that the automatic pool sweep had yet to be installed.

"That doesn't matter a bit," she said. "The only thing I care about is—can I go for a swim?"

"You sure can."

"Oh, boy!" Impulsively, she threw her arms around his neck and gave him a hug. "Let me run upstairs and put on a suit."

While changing, she had a wonderful idea. Mike might have neighbors who could look over the back fence at *his* pool, but Joanne's backyard was completely inaccessible to prying eyes. That was assuming she could get rid of any potential voyeurs *inside* the house. She found the only possible voyeur seated at the kitchen table, with an open textbook in front of him.

"Gary," she began commandingly, "you've been working too hard. I think you ought to take the rest of the day off."

He grinned naughtily. "Planning some hanky-panky in the new pool?"

"None of your business," she teased. "Some day, you and I need to have a discussion about the proper role of a housekeeper. Et cetera, et cetera."

He tugged on a lock of hair just above his forehead. "Yes, ma'am. Certainly, ma'am. Whatever you say, ma'am," he said, accompanying his words with exaggerated head-bobbings.

"Oh, go away, Gary." She laughed.

Emerging from the kitchen, she found Mike seated at the glass-topped table in the breakfast nook, doing some final paperwork.

She sat down on the chair beside him, gratified by the way his gaze lingered for a moment on her face, then swept down over her curves. Apparently, familiarity with her body had yet to induce boredom.

"So the pool's really done," she said happily.

"Yep. And in plenty of time for your party."

Since Mike had declined to attend, what would be the point of having a party? Joanne wondered.

"Oh, yeah. That isn't going to work out, after all. Too many of my friends are going to be out of town."

Mike felt momentarily uneasy. Was that the real reason she'd canceled? He'd hate to think he was coming between her and her friends. "You'll have your open house some other time, then?"

"Sure. Soon as I get around to scheduling it." She waited until he had finished with his paperwork and had put it away in his briefcase. Then she leaned toward him. "Okay, now, Mike. Show me this pool you built. I want a really good look at everything."

"You've been looking at it every single day," he laughingly protested. "You probably looked at it this morning, didn't you?"

"Well, yes. But it wasn't officially *finished* then. Now it's finished and I want to go look at it."

She rose and tugged open the sliding-glass door.

It was almost as he'd drawn it in that watercolor sketch that had so captivated her. Glowing with the rich browns and russets of late summer, the hillside sloped down to a half-concealed retaining wall built of irregularly-shaped stones. The stream purled onto the lot, with an oak hanging low over the water, and seemed— although it was the pure illusion of Mike's magic—to feed the sparkling blue of the stone-circled pool.

A hilly mound crowned with shrubbery helped conceal the pool machinery. The only obviously artificial thing was the spa, off to one side, and some shrubs and plants would eventually make its location a leafy bower of privacy. Not that there wasn't plenty of privacy already: Natural features screened the lot on two sides, and the wall that blocked off the other approaches had been raised to nearly eight feet.

It was a separate world, a world that beautifully imitated nature, yet had all the conveniences of aquatic technology. It was all Joanne had hoped for, and more—the "more" being the fact that she had never even *dreamed* of sharing this place with a man she loved.

She turned to smile at that man. "It's really beautiful, Mike. You did an absolutely fabulous job."

He still wasn't comfortable with compliments, although he had apparently learned to accept her enthusiasm about his lovemaking skills. He looked slightly embarrassed. "It'll look better when some of the plants grow taller and fill out a little more."

"I know. But that doesn't matter. It's beautiful, all the same." She looked at the pool, then back at Mike. "There's only one thing wrong with that pool, Mike Balthazar."

"Yeah, I know. The robot pool sweep isn't here yet."

"No, not that."

"What, then?"

"We're not swimming in it."

"Go ahead," he told her.

She shook her head. "You, too."

"I don't have a suit."

She reached around behind her to unhook the top of the two-piece swimsuit she had donned upstairs. "Neither will I, in a minute."

Mike's jaw dropped. "Joanne! What about Gary? He could come out any minute."

"Uh-uh." She shook her head. "I gave Gary the rest of the day off."

She had succeeded in undoing the hook of the bra part of her suit. She tugged at the bow that tied the straps behind her neck. It gave way and she let the skimpy garment drop to the deck.

Mike's gaze darkened. With one hand, he reached out to caress her bared breast, teasing her nipple so that it stood erect. With his other hand, he unbuttoned the top button of his shirt.

"Hell, give him the rest of the *week* off," he growled. "It's going to take more than one afternoon to properly inaugurate this pool."

10

THE DOORBELL RANG. With the phone cradled to her ear—and thank heaven, she'd finally had time to get her cordless one adjusted—Joanne crossed the living room. "No, I'm afraid it can't wait until next week. We're assembling the list of door prizes now." She paused. "Look, why don't you put me through to your CEO? I have a hunch he'd want to be very certain that your company's contribution was listed on the program. Don't you agree?"

She took only a perfunctory look through the peephole, instantly recognizing the sturdy shape outside that was silhouetted by the late-afternoon sun. She opened the door, thinking how silly it was of Mike not to have accepted the key she'd offered him.

She stood on tiptoe to press a kiss to his cheek, made a "Make yourself at home" gesture, then purred into the phone, "Ah, Mr. Gladstone, I'm *so* delighted you're going to be able to deal with my little problem personally."

Mike took a quick appreciative look at her. He enjoyed her when she was in her brisk businesslike mode, telling the world how it ought to run itself. Except for the fact that she had kicked her shoes off and was rubbing one stockinged foot against the calf of the other leg, she even looked all business—in another of her slim neutral-colored skirts and a tailor blouse.

He returned her kiss with a brief one dropped on her temple. Then, leaving her cajoling Mr. Gladstone out of something that Mike had no doubt the man would ultimately believe had been *his* idea to give, he strolled through to the back of the house. He was not yet tired of gazing at his pool.

As he opened the sliding-glass door, he caught himself midthought. *His* pool? Joanne's pool. It was okay for him to feel a certain degree of pride in the way it had turned out, but he had absolutely no right to feel proprietary.

He crossed the redwood deck, then followed the curving pebbled path to the pool. Standing on the flat stone edging, he looked around, smiling. But his smile faded as he focused on the automatic pool sweep and gradually realized what it was doing.

Or rather, what it wasn't doing.

The sweep had finally arrived the day before, and Mike had installed it himself. Yesterday, it had seemed to be working just fine. Today, although it was chugging back and forth, filtering debris from the water as it was supposed to, it wasn't chugging through *all* the water. It seemed to have decided to boycott the shallow end. Back and forth, back and forth it went, cleaning and recleaning not quite half the pool.

Perhaps all it needed was some simple adjustment of the pattern programmed into it, Mike decided. Planting his feet on the stonework, he leaned over the water toward the device, meaning to grab it and haul it ashore. But as if it had guessed his intention, it made a turn and chugged out of reach. Mike made one more unsuccessful grab at the pool sweep, then decided he might as well combine business with pleasure.

Joanne came out of the house just as Mike was stripping off his trousers. She always enjoyed the sight of his muscular thighs and nicely developed calves. She paused on the redwood deck, enjoying, then had a sudden thought and called, "You might not want to do that, Mike."

He turned around, clad only in his shirt and plain brown briefs. "Why not?"

Why not, indeed? She couldn't tell him he couldn't go into the water in the buff because any minute now she expected Tim and Lindsay to drop by "unexpectedly."

"Uh, Gary's here," she explained lamely.

"So?" He shrugged. "Men see other men naked in locker rooms all the time."

She walked closer to him. Perhaps if she started a conversation, he'd stop taking off his clothes. "When was the last time you were in a locker room?"

He paused, his fingers on the topmost button of his shirt. "High school," he admitted after a moment. "But I'll bet they haven't changed much since then. Still a bunch of sweaty guys snapping towels at each other."

"What sport did you play in high school?" she asked curiously. It was intriguing to think of him in a football helmet and shoulder pads. Much nicer than the funny little caps and knee-length trousers baseball players wore.

He went on unbuttoning his shirt. "I couldn't be on any of the teams," he replied in the level tone that Joanne had learned he used whenever the topic was a potentially emotional one. "I had to work after school, remember?"

Joanne sucked in her breath. Why could she never get it straight that Mike's poverty had meant that his growing-up years had been entirely different from hers? Not only had he missed out on all the after-school activities—sports, clubs, spending time with friends. But weekends, while she had played and partied and taken ballet lessons and ridden horseback, Mike had been working to bring money into the house.

He slipped his shirt off his shoulders and dropped it on top of his trousers, which lay across the white wrought-iron table. Four matching chairs with squashy white cushions were grouped around the table. Joanne planned to serve dinner out here—the impromptu meal, scraped together because Tim and Lindsay had dropped by, that Mike would never know she and Gary had planned so carefully.

Mike slipped his hands under the waistband of his briefs. His mouth curved wickedly at the corners as he thrust out a hip in a parody of a stripper's move. She liked it when he teased, even though she could guess that at this moment, it was because he wanted to change the subject, away from the hardships of his youth.

And even though it was pure mockery on his part, and she knew they wouldn't be able to do anything about it for hours and hours, Joanne felt a quiver of response low in her body. The man's appeal for her had shown no signs of wearing off, she realized. Not one tiny bit.

She decided to make a last attempt to save him from embarrassment. After that, she was going to consider the whole thing as falling under the heading Turnabout Is Fair Play. After all, Mike's son and daughter-in-law had seen a part of *her* anatomy that was usually concealed.

"If you want a bathing suit, I'll bet Gary has one he could loan you," she suggested.

He regarded her with perplexity. "What on earth is all this stuff about bathing suits? You didn't seem to care about me wearing one yesterday, or the day before, or the day before that...."

"Gary wasn't here then," she pointed out. In fact, Gary had begun complaining that he was sick and tired of being given so much time off.

"So? I'm the one stripping, not you. I'm sure Gary could care less about seeing *me* naked."

"True," Joanne was forced to agree.

Mike peeled his briefs off and stepped out of them.

"Well, if you're sure," she murmured, bemused as always by how extremely pleasant he was to look at. Not that looking was or ever would be sufficient.

As she walked over to the edge of the pool, she shrugged an "On your own head be it" shrug, which Mike seemed not to notice. He poised himself on the stone coping, then dived in, his body cleanly cutting through the water.

He came up for air, his wet hair streaming over his eyes at the exact moment when Joanne heard the glass door leading to the house slide open, then footsteps on the deck behind her.

She turned and smiled at her friends—Lindsay, cool and elegantly slim in a sleeveless pale blue dress, and brown-haired Tim, athletic looking in shorts and a tank top. "Why, Lindsay! Tim!" she crowed. "What a lovely surprise!"

Three hours later, Mike—fully dressed—glared down at Joanne with exaggerated ferocity. They stood at the foot of the stairs in the foyer, having just seen Tim and Lindsay out the front door. He said, "You know, I ought to wring your neck for that little stunt you pulled this afternoon."

Joanne batted her eyelashes and dimpled a smile up at him that would have sent a diabetic into sugar shock. "Why, whatever do you mean?" she asked in a syrupy Southern drawl.

"You set me up. You *knew* Tim and Lindsay were stopping by, didn't you?"

"Why, Mike, how could you—"

"Liar, liar, pants on fire! If you hadn't known they were coming, you wouldn't have dropped all those hints." He mimicked her with an ultrahigh soprano. "'Are you sure you want to do that, Mike?' 'You could borrow a bathing suit from Gary, Mike.'" He glowered fiercely. "Dirty, rotten . . ."

She pretended to be afraid of him. Holding her hands up, palms out, she backed up a pace. "You see? I was *trying* to save you from yourself."

He lunged toward her, a grin warring with his mock scowl. "You didn't try very hard," he protested, then made another lunge in her direction, which she evaded with some fancy footwork. "Hey!" he complained. "Stand still so I can chew you out properly!"

"No way!" Without warning, she turned and bolted up the stairs.

Taken by surprise, Mike was a little slow to follow. She reached the landing several steps ahead of him. Panting, she darted into the bedroom and tried to shut the door before he could enter, but he reached it before she got it closed all the way.

She used all her strength to keep Mike from pushing it open, well aware that he was playing a game with her; that if he exerted a fraction of his full power, he could be inside the room in an instant.

They shoved the door back and forth a few times. Then he protested through the opening, "Why didn't you just tell me you had friends coming over?"

He pushed in and she braced herself to resist, planting her feet and leaning her entire body weight against the door. "Oh, yeah? And what would you have done if I *had* told you?"

"I . . . uh . . ."

Suddenly, he stopped pushing and Joanne fell forward, slamming the door shut and barely catching herself before she fell.

She stared blankly at the barrier for a moment, then turned the knob and let him in. "Something wrong?" she asked as he walked past her into the room. "I didn't expect you to give up so easily."

He turned to face her, his hands in his pockets. "Okay. So if I'd known Tim and Lindsay were coming over, I wouldn't have stuck around."

She closed the distance between them, then placed the flat of her palms on the muscles of his chest. "And that would have been too bad, wouldn't it?"

"Maybe. I don't know."

"Maybe? You had a good time with Tim and Lindsay, didn't you?"

He shrugged.

"Well, they had a good time with you. They liked you a lot, Mike."

His face shuttered. She couldn't really blame him for being suspicious of anyone she labeled a friend. Not after that first disastrous party. "How do you know that?" he asked.

"I can tell. And besides, Lindsay told me they did." She slid her hands up his chest and over his shoulder, then linked her fingers behind his neck. "And besides *that*, why wouldn't they like you? You're a very likable guy, Mike Balthazar."

Except when you're being a stubborn, pigheaded idiot, refusing to admit that we belong together.

Mike made his usual embarrassed grimace at being complimented. Then he took his hands out of his pockets and put them on her waist, squeezing briefly before he bent to kiss her. It was like all their kisses—a dance, a duel, a communion; endlessly inventive and inevitably intoxicating.

By the time the kiss ended, Joanne was feeling an inordinate desire to press her lower body against Mike's. He seemed to have similar desires; his hands slid lower on her buttocks, pulling her tightly against him.

Her breasts flattened against his chest and she couldn't resist rubbing her upper body back and forth against his. But there was a little more she wanted to say before they got to the really good stuff. She looked up at him. "Okay, Mike. So you spent some time with friends of mine and it wasn't so bad. How about reciprocating?"

"What do you mean?"

"You've met my closest friends. How about letting me meet some friends of yours?"

"I've got a friend who'd like to meet you." He tilted his hips, the thrust of his hardness against her belly leaving no doubt exactly what he meant.

For a moment, Joanne almost abandoned the subject. It was so good, feeling his body against hers, knowing that before too much longer they would be joined in that extraordinary way, moving inexorably toward an exquisite explosion of mutual release.

But she forced herself to pull back and put a few millimeters' distance between them. She thought she had made progress today, demonstrating via Tim and Lindsay that there were parts of their worlds that *could* mesh, in addition to the highly satisfactory meshing they did in bed.

"I'm serious, Mike," she said earnestly. "I've only met Bill and Kitty once." And that, hardly under the best of circumstances. "Well, Kitty a couple more times at your office," she amended. "But I've never met any of your friends."

Two vertical lines formed between Mike's brows. "I've only met Robbie a couple of times. And Jeff not at all."

"They're away," Joanne pointed out. She had long ago decided that she would arrange for Mike to meet Jeff and renew his acquaintanceship with Robbie when the boys came home from college at Christmastime. She knew better, however, than to reveal her plans to Mike. If she did, she was bound to be treated to a Mike Balthazar lecture on how their relationship couldn't last.

Spare me, she thought. In day-to-day terms, it was going very well. It was just that Mike *expected* problems.... Expected them? Understatement! He was as convinced that problems were just over the horizon as he was that the sun would come up tomorrow morning. *More* convinced, given his fundamental pessimism.

"Anyway," she went on, "we're not talking about family right now, just about friends. So how about it? Can I meet some of the people you hang out with?"

"Hang out with?" Mike gazed at her in mock astonishment. "Where'd the sixties slang come from? You don't usually talk that way."

"It's like a rash," Joanne confided. "Usually it's dormant, but every now and then it breaks out." She balled her hand into a fist and lightly socked his upper arm. It was like socking a brick. "And you, mister, are evading answering my question."

"I don't hang out a lot," he told her.

"But you go bowling every Monday night," she pointed out. "I used to bowl, you know. It's been a long time, but I wasn't too bad in college. I suppose it comes back to you."

Mike understood what she was asking—to try to bridge some of the gap between them. He gave a slight shake of his head. Fat chance, when the gap was so wide as to be unspannable by any feat of emotional engineering that *he* could imagine. On the other hand, lately on bowling nights, he'd missed being with Joanne....

Even so, he paused. Something inside him warned him that he was making a terrible mistake, but he couldn't pinpoint what exactly was wrong with this. Finally, despite his misgivings, he slowly gave in. "Well, okay."

"ARE YOU GOING BOWLING tonight, Dad?"

Mike looked up at his daughter-in-law. Kitty had just brought him a stack of memos of the calls that had accumulated while he was out. He and the younger couple were in the same bowling league—one organized by small businesses and independent contractors in the area. But he hadn't thought about his son and daughter-in-law being there when he had agreed to take Joanne bowling.

He had never admitted to Bill and Kitty that he had gone on seeing Joanne. None of their business, he thought now.

"Yes, I am," he replied.

Kitty smiled. "Oh, good."

Mike frowned. Why was she so pleased? He was about to open his mouth to warn her he wasn't coming to bowling alone tonight when the front door opened. With the door to his own office standing wide open the way Kitty had left it, he could see a deliveryman enter, carrying a cardboard carton of office supplies. Kitty turned and went to sign on the brown-uniformed man's clipboard.

GARY OPENED THE DOOR to Mike. He had a fat textbook propped open on one arm. He scarcely looked up as he mumbled, "Hi, Mike. Sorry. I've got a test tonight on pensions, leases and deferred taxes."

"Good luck with it," Mike said.

Gary drifted back down the hall, muttering to himself, "Capitalizing a lease: bargain purchase, right of ownership, net present value . . ."

Mike stood uncertainly for a moment. He could see most of the downstairs from here. No Joanne. He peered up the stairs. Did she even know he was here? And, assuming she didn't, should he climb the stairs and surprise her? But he had never entered her bedroom without an invitation, either expressed or tacit.

He grinned. Hell! Why *not* sneak up on her? He had discovered what fun it could be to do silly things like that—to tease and play.

He removed his shoes, then tiptoed up the stairs.

He found her inside the big walk-in closet in her bedroom, peering at her reflection in the full-length mirror, her expression serious.

Forgetting he had meant to sneak up on her and grab her from behind, he said, "Hey, something wrong?"

Joanne gave a little start. "Oh, hi, Mike. No, everything's fine. I was just wondering . . ." She paused for another worried glance in the mirror. "You have to tell me the absolute truth. Am I dressed all right?"

"That's what's worrying you?"

She nodded.

He gave a little shake of his head. She looked just fine to him. But he could tell that a casual answer wasn't going to be good enough. "Stay right there," he told her, then backed up several paces so he was out of the closet and in the main part of the bedroom. "Now turn around, real slow."

She was wearing a pale yellow scoop-necked top, with knee-length denim shorts. A leather belt cinched in her narrow waist. It was ordinary, conservative attire, yet her spectacular figure and spectacular hair made looking at her a deep and gratifying pleasure.

And as he looked, he felt something inside him swell with pride. Pride that was pure possessive chauvinism—and he didn't care! He was going to feel great walking into the Dyna-bowl tonight with Joanne on his arm. She was vibrant and alive, with that glow about her he had noticed from the very first. She was obviously a very special lady and, for the time being, anyway, she was his!

"You look great," he said truthfully. "Really, really great!"

MIKE PULLED OPEN the heavy swinging door and held it for Joanne to precede him into the Dyna-bowl. Noise surrounded them: the echoing rumble of balls going down the alleys; the clatter of falling pins and the voices of people moaning about bad shots or boasting about good ones. There was a lot of conversation. The league's most recent tournament had ended a couple of weeks before and, with it over, the emphasis was on social bowling—people just having fun together.

Mike put his hand on the back of Joanne's waist as they walked along the lanes, looking for Al and his new girlfriend, Gloria. Post-tournament absences had made it possible for Mike to do some reshuffling so that Al and Gloria would be teamed with him and Joanne this evening.

He'd met Gloria several times by now and liked her. More important, Al was obviously crazy about her. Mike decided he wouldn't be one bit surprised if the two of them got married before long.

He felt a momentary pang. The thought of being settled down with one woman, in one house, with a routine and continuity, had a definite appeal. He told himself he had no right to feel envious of Al, though. It was his own fault that he was spending time with a woman he would never be able to marry.

Halfway down the lanes, he found his friends. Gloria was seated, slipping on her bowling shoes. Her long dark hair fell over her shoulders as she looked up while Mike introduced Joanne.

Gloria had a low, sexy voice. When she remarked to Joanne, "So, you're the one who's been keeping Mike so busy," it sounded highly suggestive, as if Joanne might have had him tied and bound with black leather.

Joanne, he was pleased to note, wasn't a bit fazed. "Funny," she replied, "I would have said it was Mike keeping *me* busy." She waggled her eyebrows. "But not out of trouble. Definitely not."

Al laughed. His bald dome outshone the bowling balls in the rack. "Nice to meet you, Joanne."

"Nice to meet you, too." They spoke for a few minutes longer. Then Joanne turned to Mike, who had just sat down and was removing his street shoes. "I've got to go rent myself a ball," she reminded him. The other three had brought their own. "I'll be back in a sec."

Mike hesitated with one shoe off. "I'll go with you if you want."

"No need," Joanne said blithely. "Once you're set, why don't you go get us something to drink?" They had passed a little snack shop near the entrance.

"Okay. Sure. What would you like?"

"I think I'll stick to a soft drink. I'm going to be rusty enough without a beer taking the edge off my coordination." She grinned at Gloria and Al. "You did warn these two that I might not be much of an asset tonight, didn't you?"

Al shrugged. "No problem. And fortunately for you, the stakes are low."

"Stakes? I didn't know there were any."

"Low bowler buys the others a drink when we're done," Mike told her.

"Oh, whew!" Joanne exclaimed. "I ought to be able to handle that."

Mike hid his grin. He wouldn't let on to his friends that she could probably buy the whole alley and everyone in it if she chose. He caught himself. Was he actually getting a kick out of the thought? Where had *that* come from? Was it possible that in some ways he was starting not to mind so much that she had money?

Not possible, he decided. No way. He turned back to Al and Gloria.

"Nice-looking broad," Al said admiringly.

Mike might have objected to him referring to Joanne as a "broad," except that Gloria got there ahead of him.

Directing a glance at Al, she warned, "Watch your mouth, buster!"

Al ducked his head. "Sorry." He looked at Mike and gave an elaborate shrug. "Women! They're so damned picky these days. They—"

He was interrupted as a threesome came down the stairs to the lane level—Kitty, Bill, and a woman of about Mike's own age.

Kitty and Bill greeted Al and Gloria, but the younger couple seemed most intent upon dragging the unknown woman up to Mike.

"Dad, you remember Donna, don't you?" Kitty asked. "She was at our wedding. She's a friend of my mom's."

Donna looked up at Mike. She had a slim figure, brown hair arranged in careful waves around her face, and brown eyes that looked slightly anxious—and he didn't remember her at all. The wedding hadn't been that large, either. Evidently Donna had made zero impression on him.

She extended her hand. Her voice had a faint quaver of nervousness in it. "It's so nice to see you again, Mike."

"Uh, nice to see you, too."

Kitty looked at him expectantly. "You have room on your team for Donna, don't you, Dad?"

"Well, uh . . ."

A familiar contralto spoke from behind him. "Oh, hi, Kitty. Hi, Bill!"

Mike turned, relieved to see Joanne, and so he missed the expressions on the faces of the threesome surrounding him.

But Joanne missed nothing. Kitty. Bill. And the woman of an appropriate age to be paired up with

Mike. All three of them looking at her as if she were about as pleasant a sight as the green mold that forms in the bottom of an unwashed coffee cup.

It took her less than one second flat to figure out what was going on here. Bill and Kitty had brought this woman, intending her to be a date for Mike. He had known nothing about it until she showed up. Furthermore, being a man and therefore not very smart about these things, he probably still hadn't figured out why Donna was here. So he was innocent, in one respect.

But in another, he was guilty as sin.

She plastered a smile on her face, determined to see the rest of this evening through. But there were things she had to say to Mr. Michael Balthazar. Things that were, to say the least, not pleasant.

11

MIKE WAS SMILING to himself as he steered his car out of the Dyna-bowl parking lot. He'd had a terrific evening. Contrary to what he'd feared during his worst moments of foreboding, Joanne had gotten along just great, not only with Al and Gloria, but with others of Mike's friends who had stopped by to say hello and scope out "Mike's lady friend."

She had even bowled a decent game, once she had warmed up and got back the hang of it.

Feeling pretty happy about how things had gone, Mike reached over and squeezed her shoulder affectionately. "Did you have a good time?"

Joanne kept her gaze straight ahead. If she looked at him, she might scream, and she intended to try her darndest to hang on to her dignity throughout the looming encounter. "No. Actually, I didn't," she stated in a level voice.

He jerked his head back. "But you . . . I thought . . . You seemed to be having a good time with Al and Gloria. I thought you liked them."

"I like Al and Gloria very much. They're delightful people."

"Well, then . . ."

"Tell me one thing, Mike." It was going to end up being a lot more than *one* thing by the time they were through, but there was no need for him to know that at this moment.

"Sure, but—"

"Why was Donna there tonight?"

"She likes to bowl?" Mike suggested.

"Uh-uh." Bill and Kitty and their older friend had ended up bowling in the adjacent lane. Joanne had been unable to keep from sneaking glances at them. "It was obvious that Donna had never bowled in her life, could have cared less about bowling, and will probably never bowl again as long as she lives." There was no *need* to mention the woman's record-breaking number of gutter balls. "So why do you suppose she was there?"

Mike ran his hand distractedly through his hair. "Uh, gee, I don't know. She's a friend of Kitty's. I guess she wanted an evening out."

"Oh? If that's all, then why, pray tell, did Kitty and Bill *and* Donna all keep looking at me as if I were a snail on the prize-winning petunias?"

"They didn't. They— Oh, hell!"

"'Oh, hell!' is right, Mike. They brought her for you, didn't they? They were trying to fix you up."

"Don't be ridiculous."

They reached a stoplight and he stole a glance at her. Her look of disbelief was so strong that he crumbled. "Yeah. I guess maybe that is what they had in mind," he grudgingly admitted.

It had taken him a while to figure it out. And even now, he could hardly believe that Bill and Kitty had done something so buttinsky. But it explained a lot. Why Kitty had been so pleased to hear he was going bowling tonight, for instance. And why they hadn't mentioned bringing Donna—so they could ambush him with her. Since catching him in the pool with Joanne, they must have decided he needed female companionship. Likely, they had spent the intervening time lining up a suitable candidate.

The light changed to green and Mike pressed the gas pedal. "But why are you mad at me? It wasn't *my* fault!"

"Men!" Joanne muttered angrily under her breath. What gene did they lack that prevented them from seeing the obvious?

She inhaled deeply. The restraints she had imposed upon her temper were wearing thin. "It's a simple matter of logic," she said coldly. "Kitty and Bill were trying to fix you up. They wouldn't have brought what's-'er-name, Donna, if they'd had the slightest inkling that I might be there. For that matter, they wouldn't have done it if they'd had the faintest idea that I even exist."

"They know you exist. They met you, remember?"

"*I* remember." How could she forget? It hadn't been that often in her life when she'd been caught in flagrante—with one breast hanging out. "The interesting question is why *they* don't."

She turned her head to look at him as he steered the car onto the street that led up into the canyon where she lived. "Until tonight, they didn't know you were still seeing me, did they? You've let them think that we aren't even dating anymore." She snorted. "Dating. If that's what you want to call a relationship so hot it sizzles! You're in my bed at least three nights a week, Mike. And your son and daughter-in-law haven't the faintest idea."

"I didn't think it was any of their business," he protested.

She was too angry to keep on looking at him. She snapped her gaze straight ahead. The road wound upward; dark shadows cast by trees and shrubs alternated with pools of light from the overhead fixtures. There was no moon.

"Won't wash, Mike," she snapped. "It might be true if we'd only started seeing each other last week. *Or* if I'd never met Kitty and Bill. But under the circumstances, there's only one reason why they didn't know about you and me. You led them to believe we weren't seeing each other anymore, didn't you?"

Guilt stabbed Mike in the gut—and made him defensive. Where did she get off, complaining about the way he dealt with his own family?

"I didn't see any point in making a big deal out of it," he objected. He rounded a sharp curve and started up an incline, then realized he was about to drive past Joanne's house. He braked sharply, jolting them both against their seat belts. Gritting his teeth, he began backing the car up to the curb.

"It wouldn't have been a big deal," she said. "It would have taken two words. 'I'm going out with Joanne Stephenson tonight.' Anything like that would have let them know I was still in the picture."

Mike turned the key off in the ignition. Maybe humor would deflect her—she almost always responded to it. He tried to smile. "That was more than two words, Joanne."

But tonight, she wasn't to be deflected. She was deeply angry. In the glow of the streetlight overhead, he could see the white lines beside her mouth and the blaze of fury in her enormous eyes.

"You know why you didn't tell them about me, Mike?" She didn't wait for him to answer. "Because you're ashamed. Of me. Of seeing *me*. You don't think I'm good enough for you, do you?"

"Don't be ridiculous. If anything, it's the other way around."

"No, it's not." She crossed her arms over her chest. "Okay, Mike. Time for the truth. What's the matter with me that you're ashamed for your son and daughter-in-law to know you're seeing me?"

He shook his head.

"You're not going to answer? Well, I guess I'll have to figure it out on my own, then. I've never committed a crime, so it can't be that. Is it because I'm ugly?"

"No, Joanne, for Chrissake...."

"I'm no beauty queen, I know that," she continued. "But nobody has ever suggested that it would be a service to humanity if I went around with a paper bag over my head. So it can't be because you're ashamed of the way I look."

"I told you. That's not it."

"It..." She rounded on him. "So you admit that there *is* a reason. Come on, Mike. Out with it."

He stared down at the steering wheel, wishing he could just drive away from this argument. "We come from two different worlds," he muttered in a low, strangled voice. "That shouldn't be news to you, Joanne. I've been saying it all along."

She regarded him for a long moment. Then she said slowly, "You really believe it, don't you?"

He frowned. "Believe what? That we're from two different worlds? Sure, I do."

She shook her head. "Not that. What Scott Fitzgerald wrote: that the rich are 'different from you and me.' You really think it's true, don't you?"

"Isn't it?"

She seemed not to hear him. "The thing about you is that you've taken it one step further. 'The rich are inferior to you and me.' That's what you think, isn't it?"

"I never said that," Mike protested.

"No. But you believe it." She leaned toward him. "You think I've had it easy, that I don't know what life's really all about, that I've never experienced struggle or pain."

Joanne glared at him. When he didn't reply, she was angry enough that she uncrossed her arms and poked him in the chest.

Mike felt his own anger rising. Where'd she get off, attacking him like this?

"Isn't that what you think?" She poked him again.

"It's true, isn't it?" he asked defensively.

Joanne gave a curt nod. "At least, you're admitting it."

"Well, listen, Mike. Ernest Hemmingway had an answer for Fitzgerald. The rich *are* different. They have more money. And that's about it, buster. Things that *money* can fix—yeah, we don't have to worry about them all that much. But there are plenty of other things, you know. People die—dreams die—life is disappointing. Money doesn't help that one little bit."

Later, Mike would have given anything to have kept the expression of skepticism from crossing his face. But what she was saying seemed so absurd. Of course, money helped. And without it—without at least the basics—who had the room for hope or the time to dream in?

She let out a long, weary-sounding sigh. "I saw that look on your face. You don't buy it, do you? You think all the virtues and all the strengths are reserved for people who didn't grow up with money. And *that's* why you kept our relationship secret from Kitty and Bill."

She was quick, and not only mentally but physically; he had discovered that before while chasing her, playing one of their games he had come to enjoy so much. But he had never seen her move as fast as she did now. One second, she was sitting there in the front seat of his car. The next, she had opened the door and was standing outside, leaning in through the open window.

Her voice trembled with renewed anger. "I won't be with someone who's ashamed of me, Mike. I just *won't*."

She turned her back on him and started up the steps leading to her front door.

"Joanne, wait!"

She swiveled around to face him, planting her hands on her hips. "Go away, Mike. I don't want to ever see you again."

Then she was up the steps and inside, with the door slammed behind her.

Mike sat there behind the wheel for a moment, trying to figure out what had happened. And trying to decide if he should go to the door and see if she would let him in.

But to what purpose? He couldn't in all honesty tell her she was wrong.

"Goddammit!" He slammed his hand down on the steering wheel in fury and frustration, accidentally hitting the horn, which honked loudly in the quiet canyon.

After that, there seemed to be nothing for him to do but drive away.

THANK GOD FOR eye drops! Joanne stared at herself in the mirror. She would have thought she was too mature to sob into her pillow, that she would have been able to be more philosophical about a little thing like a broken heart. But sob she had, the night before; and this morning her eyes showed the evidence. Evidence she meant to conceal before she went downstairs, because the last thing she would be able to tolerate today was sympathy from Gary. Or from anybody else, for that matter. She had to get into an "It's better this way" mode and stick to it until the worst of the hurt wore off.

Anger helped. Fortunately, she still had a large supply of that. No matter how she boiled it down—Mike Balthazar was *ashamed* of her. And that was definitely infuriating—and rightfully so.

She checked her reflection. The redness was out, just as the commercials promised.

She was on her way down the front stairs when the doorbell rang. From the kitchen came the mouthwatering aroma of frying bacon. "I'll get the door," she called to Gary.

She gazed out through the peephole. Her lips tightened.

She wrenched the door wide open and faced him like an Amazon warrior defending a stronghold. "What are you doing here?"

Mike gazed at her, seeming to size up her expression, her body language. "I, uh..." There was a pause, then he said rapidly, "The manufacturer is sending someone to repair the automatic pool sweep."

"And?"

"And what?"

"And therefore I should be expecting a pool-sweep repairman," Joanne said. "Did you come all the way over here to tell me that? Wouldn't a phone call have done?"

"It's my responsibility." Mike's jaw got that stubborn thrust she had come to know so well. "I'm in breach of contract if the sweep doesn't work the way it's supposed to. And therefore, I mean to be here to see that the repairman does his job."

Joanne gazed up at him suspiciously. It sounded fishy to her. But maybe it was legit, given Mike's exaggerated sense of responsibility. "Okay," she reluctantly agreed. "Come on in."

She stepped back a good long pace as Mike entered the foyer. She might be furious with him, but that didn't mean she was immune to his potent physical appeal. A wise woman would stay well out of range.

Mike looked at her, seeming about to speak.

The flap of a swinging door made Joanne look toward the end of the big open room nearest the kitchen. Gary stood there, wiping his hands on his apron. "Joanne, breakfast is— Oops, sorry." He turned back toward the kitchen.

Mike glanced only briefly at the retreating housekeeper before returning his gaze to Joanne's face. He had wrestled with the problem half the night—it would be wise to leave things the way they were. There was no future for the pair of them, so why *not* let her end it? He would heal. She would heal. They would both be able to move on, ultimately to someone more suited to each of them.

In that case, why was he here? And why was his mouth open? Why was he saying in tones that, to his own ears, sounded embarrassingly like a plea, "Look, Joanne, can't we forget about last night?"

She stared at him, the pupils of her eyes so wide that there was only a faint rim of blue iris around the dark centre. "I'm afraid not."

There was less anger than sorrow in her voice now, which scared Mike. She wasn't going to come around just because he wanted her to.

"But, Joanne . . ."

Her tone was adamant. "I won't sleep with someone who's ashamed to tell his own family that he's dating me."

And that was the bottom line. She didn't require that Mike take out an ad in the papers. She didn't require that he describe to Kitty and Bill the raptures of the lovemaking they experienced in each other's arms. But if he couldn't tell his own grown son and daughter-in-law that he was spending time in her company—well, that was shame, pure and simple.

She gazed up into Mike's face. His eyes were the clear transparent blue of the sky, but today, rather than windows to his soul, they seemed to be reflecting mirrors. She had no idea what he was thinking.

He asked, "Can I use your phone?"

Joanne blinked. "Sure." She gestured toward the far end of the open room, where the cordless phone sat on the small wicker table next to the windows. "Help yourself. I'll be . . ."

Her voice trailed away because she had no idea where she would be while he was making his call. Sitting down to bacon and eggs in the kitchen? Not too likely. At the moment, it seemed as if she would never be able to eat again. Her throat was choked up much too tightly to permit the passage of nourishment.

Or perhaps she would just be...gone. She didn't have to explain to Mike Balthazar where she was going and why.

"You'll be listening to me make a phone call," Mike finished for her in forceful tones. As he spoke, his arm moved—too fast for her to get away before he had her wrist imprisoned in his big hand. "Right this way," he said.

His grip on her was far from bruising, but she had no doubt that if she tried to slip away from him, he'd tighten the human handcuff in an instant.

She squared her shoulders in a grande-dame manner and said in her best accompanying grande-dame voice, "You don't have to yank me around. If you want me to eavesdrop on your phone call, I'll eavesdrop."

"Good."

He let go of her wrist, but stayed close to her all the way through the house to the phone. Too close for her comfort, because his mere physical presence stirred sensual recollections. The brush of his arm against hers brought with it a constellation of sensations that now would be nothing more than memories: his mouth, hot and demanding; his legs, all muscled iron, entwined with hers; the way he filled her and healed her and made her whole.

He picked up the phone and dialed. "Kitty, is Bill there?" A pause. "Know where he is?" Another pause. "Okay, I'll call him on his car phone. Oh, and Kitty—" he cast a meaningful glance in Joanne's direction "—ask Bill what I talked to him about, will you? It's meant for you, too." A momentary pause. "No, I'd rather not say it twice. Just ask Bill, okay?"

He hung up the phone and dialed again. "Bill? It's Dad . . . Uh-huh . . . ? You're stopped on the freeway? Good." His voice rose slightly. "We'll talk about this more later, but I just want to get something straight with you. And with Kitty, so I'll count on you to tell her what I've said. I didn't appreciate your trying to fix me up with that woman, Donna, last night."

Pause. Joanne could hear a tiny insect voice coming from the phone. It didn't sound angry, but more as if Bill was talking very fast, offering explanations.

"Yes, I do understand that you were trying to do me a good turn," Mike responded when the grasshopper voice had finished speaking. "But there were two things wrong with what you did. One of them was your fault, one of them was mine. Your fault is that you should have realized that a man my age doesn't want to be fixed up with anybody. That's the kind of choice a guy wants to make for himself. Got it?"

The grasshopper buzzed.

"Good. And now, for my fault. I should have made it clear some time back that I've been seeing Joanne. Ms. Stephenson." *Pause. Buzz.* "Yes, I know...." Mike sounded patient now. "I realize I should have told you." He cleared his throat. "Joanne's just been making that very same point." As if to himself, he muttered, "And making it quite clearly, too."

Joanne brightened slightly. He got it. He understood. But there was so much underlying this that she was terribly afraid that his phone call to his son, gratifying though it was, didn't really solve the problem.

She studied him as he listened to his son's voice. Mike was a good man and she loved him utterly, but without some major—

The breath whooshed out of her lungs as she registered the words he had just spoken...though reluctantly, as if they had been forced out of him. "Just one more thing you ought to know, Bill. I'm in love with Joanne."

He hung up the phone with a click that was a curtain on one of the greatest exit lines Joanne had ever heard.

Astonished, she stared at him. Then, pulled as if by a magnet, she stepped closer to him, close enough that she could feel the heat of his body. "Did you really mean that?" she asked in an awed voice.

He lifted his hand. It hovered above her shoulder without touching her. "Yes, dammit, I did!"

Joanne's heart did a pirouette; the smile that stretched her lips was so wide, it was almost painful. Though she might have dreamed of it in her wildest fantasies, she had never imagined she would actually hear him speak those words.

"That's . . . that's . . ." She swallowed. "I don't know what to say."

His eyes twinkled. "You, at a loss for words? I can't believe it." He put his finger under her chin and tipped her face up. "Are we friends again?"

She nodded. "I don't see why not." He had given her more than she'd hoped for.

He opened his arms and she stepped into his embrace. With her arms wrapped around his waist, she savored his strength. Then, almost as an afterthought, she looked up at him and murmured, "Oh, by the way . . . I'm in love with you, too, Mike."

A smile slowly curved his mouth. He began to bend his head, obviously intending to kiss her, but Joanne pulled away from him. "Wait a minute."

He frowned. "Something wrong?"

"No, I just think we ought to do this properly. Do you *really* have to stay to supervise that repair guy?"

Mike shook his head. "Nope."

"So it was all a ploy."

"Sure."

"I love it!" She ran her hand up his arm. "Mike, let's get out of here. Let's go somewhere for the rest of today and tonight . . . and make up properly."

His eyebrows lowered. "I have appointments—"

"Cancel them." She leaned into him, letting her hand rest softly on his belt buckle. "We need to be together,

Mike. At least, *I* need for us to be together. Here, we'll just be interrupted."

"I don't know," he said dubiously.

As if to bolster her argument, the phone rang. Joanne reached around Mike and flipped on the answering machine. "Just until tomorrow," she urged cajolingly. "We've been seeing each other for weeks and weeks and weeks and we haven't gone anywhere. Not one single place."

"Well . . ."

The expression on his face was so touching that tears almost came to her eyes. He looked as if he were considering doing something incredibly *daring*, something so extraordinary that people might gossip about it for years after.

"Yeah, okay," he agreed after a long moment. "Where do you want to go?"

Joanne thought quickly. Clearly, there was no way to get Mike Balthazar on a plane to Paris, which was the kind of beautifully impulsive thing she would have liked to do. Even suggesting the helicopter to Catalina Island might be pushing it.

But she knew another island—not a literal one, but an island of loveliness, catering to the most sensual whims anyone could have. She had never been there, but Lindsay and Tim had, not all that long ago, and she would trust their judgment. Midweek, there shouldn't be any trouble getting a reservation.

"How do you feel about surprises?" she asked Mike.

He seemed to consider. "Okay, I guess."

"Then, call and cancel your appointments. I'll go upstairs and pack, and after we run by your place, we'll be on our way."

The caller—whoever it was, Joanne had no intention of lingering to find out—had finished leaving a message. Mike picked up the phone and dialed. "Kitty? Cancel my appointments for today." There was a pause. "I don't know. Tell them I've got beriberi. Or bubonic plague." He paused for a moment. "No, don't worry. I'm not really sick. I'm taking the day off."

MIKE PUT HIS HEAD BACK and looked up at the stars. "This is amazing."

Joanne smiled lovingly at him. "It is pretty nice, isn't it?"

An hour's drive east of Los Angeles, the Inn had been designed for lovers. Its grounds had paths that rambled through a secluded wood and around the shores of a small lake. Its kitchen specialized in room service. All its rooms had balconies with hot tubs.

She looked through the steam rising from the water at her beloved seated opposite her in the hot tub. "Mike, will you do something for me?"

"Sure."

"I want to hear you say it."

"Say what?"

She pretended to pout. "You know."

"Oh, you mean what I told Bill on the phone?"

Joanne nodded. "You never did actually say it to me, you know."

"Didn't I?"

"Nope. You said it to Bill. And I said it to *you*. But you never said it to me."

"Oh. Then I suppose I probably should."

"You sure should."

A puzzled frown creased his forehead. "Now, what was it exactly that I'm supposed to say?"

"You're impossible," she teased, smiling.

"You, too," he agreed and slid over onto the bench she occupied. He curved his arm around her shoulders and stared deep into her eyes. "I'm in love with you, Joanne."

She shivered with joy. "I'm in love with you, too, Mike."

She tilted her face up toward his, inviting his kiss. His lips met hers with a gentleness unlike his usual hungry claiming of her mouth. What followed was soft nibbles and tentative touchings of tongue to tongue that elicited in her a heat that kept building and building. His fingers were as gentle as his mouth, caressing her above the water and beneath it, her breasts, her knees, her thighs. And finally his hand sought out the nub of pleasure between her most intimate folds of flesh.

No matter that the process in reaching this point had been slower than was sometimes the case. She was hotter than the water that bubbled and swished around them. And that water was starting to interfere with her pleasure, becoming a distraction rather than a sensory supplement.

She murmured, "Don't you think we might be more comfortable inside on the bed?"

"I thought you might enjoy it if we tried it in the tub."

"Let's not and say we did."

He smiled down at her. "Fine with me, but I thought women liked adventure in their lovemaking."

"You're plenty of adventure for me, big fella!" she said in a deliberately throaty voice.

They climbed out, and the cool night air added a new sensation to skins that had been heated both by water and by passion. After hastily drying, they kept their arms around each other's waists as they went inside.

There, lying on the king-size bed, Mike repeated some of the caresses he had given her underwater. But neither he nor Joanne seemed to need to be particularly experimental tonight. When he entered her, she had, as always, an overwhelming sense of completion, of wholeness, of a fitting together that was perfection. He moved within her with strong, insistent strokes that quickly brought her to the edge and propelled her over into ecstasy.

But it was a brand-new joy and relief to be able to cry out as she climaxed, "Oh, Mike, I *do* love you!"

"I love you, too," he gasped before he shuddered out his own release.

A little while later, she raised her head to look at his face resting on the pillow. His eyes were closed, his dark lashes brushing his cheeks. He looked young. Innocent. Vulnerable. And she loved him so much, her heart hurt.

"Mike?" she whispered.

At once, his eyes flew open. So he hadn't been asleep, just drifting. "Yeah?"

She touched his chest with her fingertips. "You said you loved me, right?"

He nodded.

"And I love you."

"Yeah," he answered happily.

"So, what does that mean to our relationship, Mike?"

He froze. "Mean? What do you mean?"

"I mean, are we going to change anything?"

Mike deliberately kept his expression blank. It had felt good and right to admit—to himself, to Joanne, to Bill—that he was in love with her, but he hadn't thought beyond that point. "I don't see why," he said defensively. "We've been getting along okay the way we are."

Joanne bit her lip. So he hadn't even considered for an instant that they might live together, might even . . . marry. "I guess we have," she said slowly.

It was obvious from his shuttered, remote expression that *he* wasn't going to continue the discussion. She snapped out the bedside lamp, then lay down beside him. Though she kept her face pressed into the pillow for quite some time, sleep would not come.

Finally, she rose. Slowly and quietly, so as not to disturb Mike, she slid open the door that led to the balcony and stepped outside. The stars were high and bright, pinpoints against the night sky.

Chilled, she hugged herself, then let out a deep, unhappy sigh. Perhaps the reconciliation with Mike had been a mistake. Because of it, she had another wonderful memory to add to her store of memories and perhaps, in old age, when her body's hungers were no longer so demanding, she would think of this night and be glad.

But now, all she could think of was the fact that nothing had really changed. Mike had said he loved her, and the joy of hearing those words had temporarily blotted out her common sense.

Grudging step by grudging step was the way he had entered her life. And despite everything that had happened, his resistance was still at the same level. He might love her, but he certainly had no interest in moving their relationship toward a lifelong commitment. That was fairly obvious. And this meant that, sooner or later, there would be a crisis.

She heard the door behind her open, felt a touch on her arm. "Come back to bed, Jo," he said.

She smiled at the shortening of her name. He used so few endearments that even something as innocuous as that was precious to her. She let herself slip into the circle of his arm. She should just enjoy what they had, she decided.

But she couldn't shake off a sense of imminent disaster—as if the crisis she feared might be just around the corner.

12

MIKE PARKED HIS CAR in front of Joanne's house. Their one-day idyll was over.

Back to the real world, Joanne thought. She turned to Mike. "Are you coming in?"

"Just for a minute. I want to make sure the pool sweep is working properly. But then I need to get to the office."

Joanne unlocked the front door and pushed it open. "Want something to drink?" she asked Mike as he started through the big central room to the sliding-glass doors that led outside.

"No, thanks."

The call light on her answering machine was blinking. She sighed. She got a great deal of satisfaction out of her charity work, and it was nice to be needed, but...

She rewound the tape and listened to the first one. It was a fellow committee member bemoaning a hitch in the plans for a winter fund-raiser for the Children's Hospital. The events coordinator at the hotel whose ballroom they planned to use had given their date to another organization.

Joanne pressed her lips together in a firm line. She'd take care of *that* in short order. A simple reminder to the events coordinator of how much party business she sent to that hotel, a minor threat or two...

The next call was from Warren, reporting a drop in one of the bonds she held and recommending that she sell. The next call was also from Warren, more or less repeating the same message, but adding, "Where are you, darling? Why haven't you returned my call?"

As Joanne listened, and underlined "Call Warren" on the list she was making, she looked out at the backyard. Mike stood on the edge of the pool, studying the movement of the automatic sweep. As she watched, he turned, his hand raised, thumb and forefinger forming a circle.

Joanne smiled and nodded, but her smile faded as she heard the next message on the tape, "Ms. Stephenson, it's Carrie Bestow at the Westwinds Travel Agency. There's been a slight change in the itinerary for your trip. Since your departure's only three weeks away, I thought I'd better call and discuss it with you."

Trip. Prague. The dream city she'd always longed to see. The journey she'd planned for, dreamed of. And she'd pretty much forgotten about it.

She stared straight ahead without seeing anything.

She still wanted very much to go to Prague.

But she didn't want to go without Mike.

It took her a moment to realize that the crisis she'd foreseen only the night before was already upon them.

Of course, there were things she could do to avert it. She could cancel her trip. Or she could go and when she returned, she and Mike would probably be able to pick up where they'd left off.

But there was more to it than that. This was about their relationship. People who loved each other traveled together. They didn't take separate vacations. For that matter, people who loved each other lived together—perhaps even married, if that was what both of them wanted.

She'd been fooling herself, she realized. Managing to forget about her trip was part and parcel of the same self-delusion that had let her believe—temporarily—that just because Mike Balthazar had said he loved her, everything was going to be all right.

Well, it wasn't going to be all right. Not all right at all, she thought bleakly.

The sliding-glass door opened and Mike came in. "Works like a charm," he reported. Then he zeroed in on Joanne's face. "Something wrong?"

"Not wrong, exactly," she answered carefully. "Uh, can I get you a cup of coffee, Mike? I need to talk to you about something."

He frowned. "I need to get back to work, but I guess one cup wouldn't hurt."

She went into the kitchen, where, as she'd confidently expected, Gary had a pot of coffee made. The door to his room was open and her housekeeper was sitting at his desk, studying. As her footsteps crossed the tile floor, he turned his head and smiled at her, a greeting on his lips. But one look at her expression silenced him.

He frowned, then questioned her with lifted brows.

She began softly, "I know I've been asking this a lot lately, Gary, and I'm sorry—but could you possibly find some errands to run?"

"Sure." He must have gathered that it wasn't hanky-panky in the pool or anywhere else that she had in mind this time. He added quietly, "Another fight, already?"

Joanne considered for a moment. "I don't know if it's going to be a fight or not," she said. "Probably."

The *last* fight was what her intuition suggested it was bound to be. She couldn't imagine she had much hope of winning this one.

That meant that she and Mike were both going to lose—and lose big.

And yet she had to do it. She had no choice.

"Let's just say that I think complete privacy would be in order," she told Gary.

"Say no more." He rose and closed his book, then came out of his room and walked across the kitchen toward her. "I need to go to the library anyway." When he reached her side, he suddenly bent over and dropped an affectionate kiss on her cheek. "Good luck, Joanne. I hope it turns out okay."

"Thanks, Gary." She let out a long sigh. "Me, too."

When she emerged from the kitchen, carrying two steaming cups of coffee, she found Mike seated at the breakfast table. He was just hanging up the phone. "I was calling Kitty at the office," he explained. "Hope you don't mind."

"No, of course not."

As she put one of the cups in front of him, he said, "Thanks," then, "There was something you wanted to talk to me about?"

Joanne sat down and crossed one shaky leg over the other. "Yes," she said gravely. "I don't know how to explain this, Mike, because I don't understand it myself, but there's something I'd completely forgotten about... The trip I'm going on in a few weeks. To Prague."

His face was unrevealing. He ran the tip of one finger over the handle of his cup. "Oh, yeah. I remember you talking about how much you'd always wanted to go there. Your trip is coming up that soon?"

She nodded. "I'll be gone for a month, Mike."

His face went through a series of expressions too quickly for Joanne to be certain she was reading any of them correctly. Dismay, maybe. A brief flash of anger—*perhaps*.

Then he said equivocally, "That's a long time."

"Yes." She drew a deep breath. "Now, don't say anything. Just think about this for a minute. I'd like you to go with me, Mike."

She looked into his eyes and saw him shutting down and shutting her out. He wasn't going to think about it, not for one instant.

She went desperately on, knowing that nothing she said was going to make any difference, but having to say it all anyway so that later, she could tell herself she had given it her very best shot.

"I realize that maybe there are other parts of Europe you'd rather see than Czechoslovakia. I don't even mind changing my plans. As long as I get to spend a *little* bit of time in Prague, we can certainly do other things. None of the distances are very far over there, compared to here. We could go to Vienna. Rome. Paris. Anywhere you like. We could—"

He cut her off. "Joanne, stop it!" He pushed his chair back from the table. She wouldn't have been surprised if he'd risen and walked out on her. But having increased his distance from her, he remained seated. "It's out of the question and you know it."

She picked up her cup, then set it down again. "No, I don't *know* anything of the kind. What's out of the question about it?"

"I can't afford it," he said flatly.

"Look, if it's money, then, hey!" She smiled, trying to keep it light. "It's on me, okay?"

She'd known he wouldn't like her offering to pay. But it was something she'd *had* to say, to get through the layers of Mike's defenses to the real issues underneath.

He didn't like it.

His face went dark. "Not okay!" His voice was soft but frightening, like the low rumble just before an earthquake hits full force. "If I *were* going to take a trip like that, I'd pay my own way."

Again he pushed his chair back, away from her. And this time, he did stand. Resting his palms on the table, he loomed over her. "But it's a moot point and you ought to know it. I can't just up and leave like that. There are projects we're in the middle of. The business doesn't just run itself, you know."

"But you have a grown son to help run it," Joanne pointed out. "Besides, you'd have three weeks before we leave, to get things organized. And there are phone lines between Europe and here."

He shook his head. "It's impossible."

She had a momentary cowardly impulse to leave it at that. Their relationship might still be salvageable if she did. But she couldn't let it lie. She had intended to get to the fundamental issues and now she was near them. She couldn't back off. "It's not impossible," she insisted. "If you really wanted to do it, you could."

His mouth twisted. "You know what the trouble with you is? You're spoiled. You think you can have everything exactly the way you want it. Well, life isn't like that, baby. Not for most of us poor working schlubs."

Here they were, at the crux of the matter. She pushed her own chair back and rose, needing to be on a more equal footing with him. "Oh, no? What *is* life like, Mike? Since you seem to have the corner on the answers."

"It means being responsible."

"And I'm not?"

"No, you're not. You wouldn't know what the word means." Mike knew, even as he spoke, that he was distorting the truth. He had seen her day after day, steadily and reliably working for the charities she supported. But he was wound up into something here, trying to make his point, and a little thing like pausing to consider the truth was beyond him.

She drew herself up to her maximum height. "You're full of it, Mike Balthazar. Absolutely full of it!" She glared at him for a moment, then exhaled a long, painful breath. "Okay, Mike, you did it. You win."

Mike was puzzled. What was there for him to win here? Her agreement that he couldn't possibly go with her to Europe was the only thing he could think of, but her tone didn't sound as if she meant *that*. "What are you talking about?"

Her voice vibrant with emotion, she flung at him, "You decided, day one, that it wouldn't work between us. And ever since, you've been making sure that it wouldn't. I don't know why, exactly, you had to do that, but I do know one thing: I give up. I'm sick of fighting you. I love you, but I *quit!*"

His jaw dropped. Before he could say anything, she went on, "You were right. We can't possibly have a relationship . . . just like you've been saying all along. It's over, Mike. And this time, I really mean it. Saying a few words—even wonderful words like 'I love you'—isn't going to change anything."

He stood there with his mouth open. Now that she had said what she had to say, Joanne thought it a pity that she couldn't walk out and slam the door behind her. In her own house, though, it might end up making her look pretty silly.

But there was nothing more to be said. She might as well head upstairs. She would be nearer to her pillow, which she had a hunch was due to get a whole lot more cried upon than it had been already.

Mike trailed behind her as she walked to the front of the house. He still hadn't said a word since her outburst. At the foot of the stairs, he paused and watched her mount the steps.

Halfway up, she turned and looked down at him. "I assume," she said imperiously, "that you'll be able to let yourself out."

MIKE HAD NO IDEA where he was going when he drove away from Joanne's house, but he ended up at the office.

Bill was there, sitting in the chair next to Kitty's desk when Mike walked in. And all at once, Mike wished he had gone somewhere else—anywhere else. Surely the two of them would see the pain etched on his face and pity him.

He grunted a hello, then hurried past into his private office.

For a while he sat, staring at his blotter. There was an ink stain on it that reminded him of a dollar sign. If it hadn't been for Joanne's money...

That thought seemed fruitless and he hadn't gotten anywhere pursuing it when there was a knock on the door.

Before he could say "Come," Bill was inside. His jaw was set, his face strangely familiar in a way that was new to Mike. And then he realized that all of a sudden, his son's face resembled the one he himself confronted in the mirror each morning.

He swallowed, willing himself to hide his pain. "Problem?" he asked.

"Yes," Bill stated firmly. "I'm here to tell you that I can't work with you anymore, Dad. I'm going out on my own."

Mike sat bolt upright. "Wha-a-at?" Was the world falling apart? How could all these things be happening at once? "What are you talking about? Why would you do that?"

"I have to," Bill said stubbornly.

"Is this Kitty's idea?"

Bill sat down stiffly. "No."

"But why?"

"You know, I told you we've been seeing a marriage counselor?"

Mike nodded.

"Well, Kitty doesn't like the way she bosses me around any more than you do. Or I do. But she can't stop doing it—and I can't stand up to her—as long as I'm working with you."

"What in hell are you talking about?"

Bill drew a deep breath, then said forcefully, "You don't trust my judgment, Dad. You don't let me supervise any of the work on my own. You keep me under your thumb all the time. How do you expect my wife to treat me like a man—how do you expect me to see *myself* as a man?—when every day you treat me like a kid?"

"I don't—" Mike began.

"You do," Bill insisted. "Kitty feels it. I feel it. It's not the only reason why she and I have the problems we do, but it sure doesn't help! The marriage counselor agrees. I've got to get out from under your thumb."

Mike stared dumbly at his son. "But the business . . . It's for *you*. It'll be yours someday."

"And maybe someday I can come back and work with you. But first, I've got to get out and do some things on my own. Establish my independence. Convince myself—and you—that I'm a grown up."

Mike sat silent for a long, long moment, his mind racing a zillion miles a minute. Then he said, "I can see we need to do some talking, son. Maybe a lot of talking. Maybe a lot of straightening things out and learning to understand each other better. But I don't think there's any need for you to leave the business." He saw Bill's look of denial and held up a hand to stop him from speaking. "Before you say anything, let me tell you what I have in mind. . . ."

"I'M SURVIVING," Joanne said briskly into the phone in response to Lindsay's worried question. It was four days since she had expunged Mike Balthazar from her life. And it was true—she *was* surviving. Wetly—in terms of the gallons of tears that had soaked her pillow. And thinly—she was lucky when she could manage to choke down a few bites of food. But she was indeed surviving. Time would pass, and bit by bit she would feel better.

She forced a laugh. "If it gets too bad, I can always jump out a window while I'm in Prague. Just kidding!" she added when she heard her friend's wordless exclamation. "Honest, Linds. Don't worry about me. I'll be fine."

And she would. Eventually. Once she'd managed to forget all about what might have been.

THE CLOCK ON MIKE'S DESK said eleven. Outside it was dark. He had been sitting in his office for hours, going over the company books. He and Bill had talked a lot during the past few days and one of the promises he'd made his son was that, in addition to giving Bill additional responsibility and independence, he would teach him more about the company's financial position.

It was, when he looked at it all laid out on paper, not too bad.

Damn good, in fact.

Mike's own personal bankbooks were in the drawer with the company financial records. Curious, he got them out and added up the amount notated in his savings passbook, the balance in his checking account, and other sums he'd invested in blue-chip stocks and bonds. The total astonished him.

It wasn't anything like what Joanne was worth, of course, but they weren't in competition and never had been.

MIKE WAS LATE REACHING the office the next morning. He'd started doing some thinking and once started, couldn't stop until the small sad hours of the morning.

Kitty looked up as he entered. Her face looked softer, he noticed, and her eyes had a shine that might have been happiness.

"Dad, could I talk to you for a minute?" she asked.

"Sure." He dropped into the chair beside her desk.

She folded her hands in front of her. "I just wanted to thank you for what you're doing for Bill. I . . ." She looked away, focusing on the fluffy little kitten on the calendar on the wall opposite her desk. "I don't like to be so bossy with him, but . . ." She blinked. "Well, it's complicated."

"I know." In a version that Bill had warned his father was highly oversimplified, he had explained to Mike that Kitty's own father had been so weak and ineffectual that her mother had had to take charge or else no decisions would ever have been made. Kitty didn't *want* her marriage to be a replay of her own parents' miserably unhappy one, but there had been times when she had felt trapped into repeating the same scenario.

Hearing Kitty's history, Mike had realized that he had been foolish to fear that Joanne would ever have bossed him the way Kitty did Bill. She was a different person, with a different personality and a different background.

"I understand," he told Kitty now.

"Thanks, Dad," she said warmly. Then her tone turned solemn. "Bill told me you're not seeing Mrs. Stephenson anymore."

"That's right."

"I'm sorry. But in the long run, it's probably for the best."

"Yeah, I guess," he agreed, then frowned. "Wait a minute, Kitty. *Why* is it for the best that we're not seeing each other? From your point of view, I mean."

She shrugged. "You know...."

"No, I don't know." He used to know, but for some reason he'd forgotten—after a week of lonely nights—exactly why it was so much better this way. "Not anymore."

Kitty spoke it as if it were self-evident: "You and Mrs. Stephenson, you don't have anything in common. You're from two different worlds."

Exactly what he had said to Joanne, over and over again. Rubbing it in. Beating her over the head with it.

And at this moment, he wasn't even certain he believed it.

Gently, he said, "We're all from different worlds, when you come right down to it." He'd never been one given to philosophical utterances, but he sensed he was on the verge of figuring out something important.

"What do you mean?"

"Well, you and Bill, for instance. Your childhood was a lot different from his."

"Uh-huh."

"So sometimes it's hard for you to understand each other, isn't it?"

Kitty nodded. "It sure is."

"So, in that respect, even though neither one of you grew up rich, the two of you came from different worlds, didn't you?"

"I guess."

"Well, what I've figured out is that we all do. When it comes to the bottom line, no two people come from the same world, Kitty. No two people are really alike. We're all different from each other. We're all separate. And ultimately, each one of us is alone. But the thing is this—it's enough if we can reach out and touch each other across the gap. Enough! Hell! It's terrific! Amazing!"

Amazing indeed, he reflected.

And he had almost failed to see the simple yet profound significance of the way he and Joanne were with each other, the way they were able to close the gap and become, at times, not two alone, but one together.

Leaving his daughter-in-law to stare in astonishment after him, Mike rose, bemused, and made his way into his office.

Okay, Mike. So you've figured it out—finally! What the hell are you going to do about it?

JOANNE LOOKED AT her packed bags set side by side in the foyer. She refused to conform to the stereotype of the affluent traveler schlepping her entire wardrobe with her, threatening porters worldwide with hernias and slipped disks. Ready to go first thing in the morning were two compact, squashy fabric suitcases and a small maroon carry-on filled with emergency items in case, as had been known to happen, her luggage vacationed in Pakistan while she was in Prague.

Still in the foyer, she checked her purse for perhaps the fifteenth time to make sure her passport, airplane tickets, traveler's checks and itinerary were all where they belonged. They were. She left the purse next to her baggage.

Back in the breakfast area of the house, she looked at her list of things to do. Solid black, triumphant lines were drawn through most of the items. All her various jobs and duties were covered for the next month.

The only thing left uncrossed out was a pleasure, not a chore. "Call boys." She would have remembered to telephone her sons, anyway—she spoke with each of them at least once a week—but she had been in a mood, when making the list, to put down absolutely everything.

Well, not *everything*, she admitted. An item conspicuously absent was what to do about eradicating all traces of Mike Balthazar from her mind and heart.

What she would have liked to be able to write down on a list was, "Ask Mike to come and take his pool away." Most mementos of a relationship could be thrown out, given away, or returned to the giver, but not the one he had left behind. Every time she looked out a window into her backyard, there was his handiwork—wrong word; there was his artistry, his creation—reminding her of the man and how the two of them had been together.

She was almost tempted, when she got home from Prague, to call a wrecking crew and have them fill the darned pool up with dirt and start all over again. Only she couldn't do that, of course. It would be wasteful. And it would mean that Mike was right in what he evidently thought of her—she really was spoiled.

She picked up the phone and dialed. She reached Jeff in his dorm just as he was about to go out to a movie with friends, but he promised to call her back later on. He would. Both boys were good about things like that. Both were, for that matter, good boys.

She dialed Robbie's number next. He was living in an apartment off campus, no more the shining academic star this semester than he'd been last year or the year before. He'd taken Mike's information about apprenticeship programs with him to college and she had a feeling that before *too* much longer, he might use it.

Robbie answered the phone after shouting, "Hey, cool it, guys!" to mute the noise his roommates were making. "So you're off tomorrow," he said. "Are you all packed? You got a ride to the airport?"

They talked about her travel arrangements for a while. Then Robbie asked, "Say, how's Mike doing?"

Joanne had been dreading that question. "Okay, I guess."

"You *guess?*" Robbie demanded astutely.

"I'm not seeing him anymore."

"Oh." Robbie was silent for a moment. "That's too bad, Mom. He seemed like a good guy."

"He was," Joanne said sadly. "He really was—is," she amended, realizing she'd spoken as if Mike were dead.

After she hung up, she wandered into the kitchen. It was one of Gary's evenings for class, so he had left her a casserole in the refrigerator. And on top of the casserole was a note.

How sweet of Gary, she thought as she read it. "In case I don't see you before you go, don't worry. I'll hold the fort. P.S. Trust me. You're going to have a perfectly marvelous time."

She didn't know why he was so sure, when she was less than certain herself, but by God, she decided, she was going to try! Never mind that she was suffering from a broken heart, she was still going to enjoy seeing Prague.

13

WITH HER MAROON carry-on bag hanging from the strap over her shoulder, Joanne walked briskly past the ticket counters where people were lined up, checking their baggage. She had already dealt with her suitcases, having handed them over to the curbside porter. Now all she had to do was get to the departure lounge and wait and wait and wait for her flight to board.

But to get to the lounge, she had to go through Security. Blocking off the concourse were four X-ray machines and four gates, manned and womanned by four sets of guards. There were lines in front of each of the machines. Joanne was too engrossed in trying to guess which line was likely to move the fastest to notice the man coming toward her until he was almost upon her.

And then she saw him and her eyes widened and her heart skipped a beat.

Quickly, she caught herself and forced onto her features a level, unrevealing expression. "Hello, Mike. You came to see me off?" She concluded that Gary must have told him her flight number.

He shook his head. "Nope."

She frowned. It was a pretty big coincidence, then, that had gotten Mike Balthazar to the airport at the moment she happened to be departing. "But I don't..."

Then she noticed he had something in his hand. A brightly colored folder like the one stuffed deep in the zippered compartment of her purse.

An airplane ticket?

A miracle had taken place and Mike Balthazar, the man who *knew* beyond a shadow of a doubt that he and she were wrong for each other, had changed his mind in a big way.

But she wasn't sure enough of that miracle to risk making a fool of herself. "You're going someplace?" she asked.

"To Prague. Assuming I'm still invited to join you." He curled his fingers around her upper arm and steered her forward into one of the security lines. "Well, actually, it looks like I'm going even if I'm not invited. I've got my airplane ticket—to Frankfurt, connecting to Prague, the same as yours. And I've got my passport and visa—it took some doing to get those, by the way. And I've got reservations at the same hotel in Prague where you're staying. So even if you don't want me traveling with you, I'm afraid you're going to bump into me from time to time." He grinned. "You can blame Gary for some of it. He makes a damned good spy, it turns out."

Unbelievable... Someday soon, she'd want to hear from Mike exactly what had happened that had made him change his mind, including every twist and turn of his thoughts. But for now it was enough to know that he *had* changed it.

Or almost enough. There were one or two things about this decision of his that she had to find out before she could give in to the joy.

She swallowed hard, scarcely noticing that the line was moving forward rapidly. "Does this mean you've changed your attitude about us?"

"Yes and no," he answered judiciously.

"Let's move it, folks!" Joanne looked up to see a woman built like a linebacker gesturing them to put their carry-on bags on the belt that traveled through the X-ray machine. Joanne dumped her purse and maroon bag on the belt, then walked through the gate, followed by Mike.

As they walked through the concourse, Joanne drew a deep breath, then looked up at Mike. "Yes and no?" she questioned.

"I still think we come from different worlds," he told her. "And I think there are problems we're going to have to work out. But I think we *can* work them out if we try. And from my point of view, it's sure worth trying." His expression grew earnest. "Do you want to try, Joanne? Or have you completely given up on me?"

"Given up on you?" She felt dizzy with astonishment and delight. "Of course not! Don't be silly!" She *had* given up; she had meant what she'd said about refusing to fight him anymore. But he didn't have to know that.

He put his arm around her and pulled her against him. Her carry-on slammed into his side and she moved away for a moment to readjust it, so they could walk the rest of the way to the gate with her snuggled right under his arm. It wasn't enough, just feeling his body against hers. Nowhere near enough, after the days and days of heartbreak and deprivation. But, for the time being, it would have to do.

They would need to do a lot of talking, she realized. Baring their souls, so that they could thoroughly understand each other and learn that in the ways that counted, they *weren't* different.

And then she glanced up at him. His eyes met hers and she had a strong hunch that he'd realized that, anyway; that he wouldn't be here otherwise.

She wasn't sure exactly what they talked about as they walked the rest of the way to the gate, their conversation continuing as they found two adjacent chairs and sat down. But it was necessary and healing talk, their way of reaching each other again, after the hurt they'd mutually inflicted and suffered.

As the departure lounge began to fill up, Mike told her how close Bill had come to walking away from the business. "It seems to mean a lot to him that I've left him in charge for the next month," he finished.

"I'm sure it does."

"But after we get back, I'm going to have to keep an eye on myself to keep from treating him like a little boy." Mike shook his head ruefully. "I didn't even know what I was doing."

"It's hard to realize our children have grown up." She grinned impishly. "Of course, mine haven't. They're still just babies."

Mike laughed. They were still talking about their children when over the intercom came the announcement: "Passengers on Flight Seven Thirty-two to Frankfurt, we will begin boarding shortly. Passengers requiring special assistance or small children traveling alone, please . . ."

Joanne squeezed Mike's hand, then disentangled her fingers from his so she could fish her ticket out of her purse. She had just gotten the folder out when the general boarding announcement was made. People rose, picked up their carry-on bags and began to funnel toward the door that led to the plane.

They were deep in conversation as the attendant pulled their boarding passes, returning a stub to each of them.

Eventually they reached the plane itself. The attractive chestnut-haired stewardess standing a few feet back from the open doorway glanced at Joanne's boarding pass. "Sixty-seven A," she said, pointing down an aisle to Joanne's right. "Down that way."

She didn't see Mike's expression as she turned in the direction the stewardess had indicated. But she did hear the young woman's voice as she checked his boarding pass. "First class, sir. That's to your left."

Joanne spun her head around. "First class?"

"I thought . . ." His rueful grin seemed about to split his face in two. "I thought for sure you'd be in first class."

"Are you kidding?" Joanne asked incredulously. "First class costs a fortune." She giggled. "I don't know whether I ought to get involved with someone so extravagant, Mike!"

The stewardess cleared her throat. "Excuse me . . ."

Other passengers pressed upon them from behind. In an instant, Mike would have to leave her and go up to the first-class compartment. But for a moment longer, they were still together. "About being 'involved' with me," he said.

"Uh-huh . . ."

"Well, I was thinking that we might as well go all the way and get married." With that, he turned and left her.

Talk about exit lines! That was the best one yet! Joanne thought as, dazed, she made her molasses-paced way up the aisle to her own seat in economy.

Meanwhile, Mike flagged the first-class stewardess. "I've got a deal for the person in seat Sixty-seven B," he told her, then explained the seat swap he had in mind. The stewardess, a Nordic blonde with classic cheekbones, gazed at him in astonishment. "You wish to trade your first-class seat for one in economy?"

"Yes, that's what I want."

"I'm sure it can be arranged, sir," replied the stewardess, as if accustomed to humoring crazy people. "But you'll have to wait until after we take off."

OUTSIDE THE WINDOW on Joanne's left, blue sky and white clouds streamed past. On the TV screen at the front of the cabin, a filmed stewardess demonstrated how Joanne could convert her seat cushion into a "flotation device." As soon as the lecture was over and the Fasten Seat Belt sign had been turned off, she intended to make her way forward to first class and have a few words with Mr. Mike Balthazar.

THE MOMENT THE SAFETY lecture was over, Mike rose. The stewardess he'd spoken to earlier was nowhere in sight. No matter, he thought. He'd just speak directly to the person in seat sixty-seven B. No need, really, to get the stewardess into the act.

He entered the first of the economy sections. A check of the numbers on the seats he was passing told him that Joanne must be in the next section back. And then he saw that the stewardesses had started beverage service. A loaded cart, with a blue uniformed woman at either end of it, blocked the aisle between him and the woman he loved.

Frowning, he glanced across the cabin at the aisle on the other side of the plane. That one was still unblocked. He retraced his steps, crossed over in front of the line of four rest rooms located between first class and economy, and again headed toward the back of the plane.

JOANNE STARED AROUND the first-class cabin. Now, where the heck was Mike? When she stood, she had spotted the beverage cart in the aisle, so she had made a crossover at the back of the plane and gone up the aisle on the opposite side from her seat.

One first-class seat was unoccupied. Mike's, undoubtedly. A stewardess with her glossy black hair pulled back into a neat bun, looked at Joanne with some suspicion, as if she might be up to something nefarious in the first-class cabin. "Can I help you?"

"The gentleman who was seated here," Joanne said. "Was he dark-haired and . . . er, extremely well-built?"

"I'm afraid I really wouldn't know."

"You probably don't know where he went, either, then," Joanne murmured.

"I'm afraid not."

Resisting the temptation to suggest that he might have stepped out, Joanne said, "Thanks," and turned to face the back of the plane.

Really, there were only two places Mike *could* have gone, she decided. Back to visit her in economy, or to the rest room.

Deciding to opt for the former, she turned and started back into the first of the economy compartments. Halfway through the cabin, she spotted Mike. He was coming toward her, but on the other side of the plane, in the opposite aisle.

He saw her at the same moment she saw him and stopped still. Over the heads of the people seated four abreast in the center part of the cabin, he called, "Hi! I've just been looking for you."

"You found me. Sort of," Joanne called back.

A man with his head snuggled down against a pillow opened his eyes and glared up at Joanne. She grimaced meaningfully at Mike. He nodded, then pointed toward the front of the plane. Realizing he must be suggesting they rendezvous at the crossover point where the rest rooms were, she turned and retraced her steps.

They met in the center of the plane. A middle-aged woman stood outside one of the rest-room doors, waiting. Another couple of people hovered nearby. But none of them seemed to pay much attention as Mike pulled Joanne to him and gave her a hug.

She gazed lovingly up at him, then lifted her brows inquiringly. "Was I hallucinating, or did you really say what I thought you said?"

His blue eyes twinkled. "What was that?"

"About us getting married."

The door of one of the rest rooms opened and the gray-haired gentleman who emerged gave the two of them an interested look before passing by to the aisle.

"Well, yeah. That is what I said." His expression sobered. "But listen, Joanne. There's one condition: We're going to have to have a very long conversation about money. Probably more than one. And we may even have to get some lawyers involved. Because I'm not going to take a penny of what's yours, no matter what. Got it?"

Joanne nodded. It might be complicated to work out, but they would manage.

"Got it," she agreed.

"Good. In that case . . ." He paused. "I just realized. I didn't ask you, did I? If you even *wanted* to get married?"

"Oh, I want to," she said. "I want to, very much."

She had never thought she would reply to a proposal outside a line of rest rooms on an airplane. And, if she'd had a choice, she would have preferred somewhere more private. For Mike was looking down at her now, with a light in his eyes that told her he was planning to kiss her—which was exactly what she wanted him to do.

Another of the washroom doors opened and out came a young woman carrying a toddler in her arms. Mike cast a quick glance at the open door, then grabbed Joanne's arm. Backing into the tiny cubicle, he pulled her inside with him. Then he reached around behind her and pulled the door shut. Before Joanne could speak, or even breathe, his arms were around her.

He bent his head. His mouth came down hard and possessively on hers. Her lips parted and his tongue slipped into her mouth. It felt to Joanne as if it had been forever, instead of only weeks, since they'd kissed. And it took only an instant for every fiber of her body to flare with desire for him.

She slid her arms around his neck, kissing him back as greedily as he was kissing her. And against her lower body, she could feel him growing, swelling—a sensation that inflamed her own passion a thousandfold.

The kiss finally had to end so they could breathe. Mike lifted his head, but he didn't release her.

With her body pressed tightly against his, she asked, "Mike, um, have you ever heard of the Mile-High Club?"

"Sure. People who've made love on airplanes, right?" His eyes widened. *"No!"*

"No?" she echoed teasingly.

He grinned. "I didn't mean 'No.' Just no, as in, 'Do you think it's possible?'"

"I don't know," Joanne told him. She looked around. There was so little space in the cubicle that Mike's knees were already backed up against the edge of the toilet. "I'm just not sure—"

She broke off as she felt Mike's fingers fumbling with the top button of her blouse. "We could give it a try and find out," he suggested.

"I suppose we could," she agreed breathlessly.

He unfastened her buttons in record time, then parted the sides of her blouse. His gaze dwelled raptly on her lace-covered breasts. "Oh, God, I've missed this," he murmured as, with his thumbs, and fingertips, he teased her nipples into hardness.

"Not half as much as I have," she whispered. She was not idle as Mike touched her, but renewed her acquaintance with his back, his buttocks and his chest, finally slipping her fingers between the buttons of his shirt to caress his hair-roughened skin.

Breathing unsteadily after another searing kiss, Joanne pulled out the tails of her blouse, then reached behind her to undo her bra. She pushed it up out of the way and, blatantly, wantonly, cupped his hands under her breasts, offering herself to him.

Mike inhaled sharply, then bent his head, inclining his mouth toward one of her nipples. But his leaning over made his shoulder collide with the wall of the cubicle. "This is a little awkward," he muttered. His eyes lit up. "Ah . . . I've got it!"

He sat down on the closed toilet, then put his hands on Joanne's waist to draw her nearer. Seated, he leaned forward, fastening his lips on her breast. With the suction, Joanne felt as if streams of molten fire were racing through her body. Her head dropped back, bumping lightly against the wall of the cubicle.

With that, Mike pulled back and looked up at her. "Jo?"

"Uh-huh."

"Any ideas on how we're going to manage actually making love?"

She tried to visualize climbing on Mike's lap, facing him while he remained seated on the commode, but an instant's thought told her that there would be no place for her knees. Standing was out; there was too great a disparity in their heights.

Maybe if —

No, she couldn't possibly sit on the sink. Even if there *were* room, which there probably wasn't, she doubted that the fixture was designed to take her weight. What would happen if the thing fell off the wall? And how on earth would they explain?

She gave a rueful shake of her head. "I haven't the faintest idea. Obviously, those Mile-High Clubbers are smarter — or better contortionists — than we are."

"I'm afraid you're right."

"There are things we could do about it, of course." She reached down and put her hand on the fly of his trousers to demonstrate what she had in mind. He was fully erect and seemed to throb under her touch.

"I know," he said, then grinned wickedly. "This may sound like a dumb idea, but it *might* be fun to wait until we get to Prague."

Joanne considered. "We'll spend the whole trip being hot and bothered."

"I know."

"By the time we get to Prague, we'll be crazy, absolutely out of our minds, wanting each other."

"We sure will," he agreed fervently.

Joanne rolled her eyes. "It sounds wonderful."

And what a way to spend her first few hours in the city she'd always dreamed of visiting—in passionate connection with the man she loved.

He rose and stood there until she'd straightened and refastened her bra and blouse. Then he bent and kissed her once more, his palm cupping her breast. "Just so you don't forget," he said.

She inclined her hips, pressing herself against his lower body. "Just so *you* don't."

It was impossible to turn around in the tiny cubicle. Mike reached behind her and slid open the lock. The door opened and Joanne backed out, nearly bumping into an elderly woman who was waiting in line for the rest room.

Joanne turned. "I'm sorry," she apologized. She registered woman's look of shock and censure at seeing two grown people of opposite sexes emerging from the cubicle together.

Joanne grinned up at Mike, then took his hand. "It's okay," she assured the older woman. "We belong to each other."

Mike's smile was wide. In his blue eyes was joy Joanne had never seen before. "The lady's right," he agreed. "We sure do!"

HARLEQUIN®
OFFICIAL SWEEPSTAKES RULES

NO PURCHASE NECESSARY

1. To enter, complete an Official Entry Form or 3" × 5" index card by hand-printing, in plain block letters, your complete name, address, phone number and age, and mailing it to: Harlequin Fashion A Whole New You Sweepstakes, P.O. Box 9056, Buffalo, NY 14269-9056.

   No responsibility is assumed for lost, late or misdirected mail. Entries must be sent separately with first class postage affixed, and be received no later than December 31, 1991 for eligibility.

2. Winners will be selected by D.L. Blair, Inc., an independent judging organization whose decisions are final, in random drawings to be held on January 30, 1992 in Blair, NE at 10:00 a.m. from among all eligible entries received.

3. The prizes to be awarded and their approximate retail values are as follows: Grand Prize — A brand-new Mercury Sable LS plus a trip for two (2) to Paris, including round-trip air transportation, six (6) nights hotel accommodation, a $1,400 meal/spending money stipend and $2,000 cash toward a new fashion wardrobe (approximate value: $28,000) or $15,000 cash; two (2) Second Prizes — A trip to Paris, including round-trip air transportation, six (6) nights hotel accommodation, a $1,400 meal/spending money stipend and $2,000 cash toward a new fashion wardrobe (approximate value: $11,000) or $5,000 cash; three (3) Third Prizes — $2,000 cash toward a new fashion wardrobe. All prizes are valued in U.S. currency. Travel award air transportation is from the commercial airport nearest winner's home. Travel is subject to space and accommodation availability, and must be completed by June 30, 1993. Sweepstakes offer is open to residents of the U.S. and Canada who are 21 years of age or older as of December 31, 1991, except residents of Puerto Rico, employees and immediate family members of Torstar Corp., its affiliates, subsidiaries, and all agencies, entities and persons connected with the use, marketing, or conduct of this sweepstakes. All federal, state, provincial, municipal and local laws apply. Offer void wherever prohibited by law. Taxes and/or duties, applicable registration and licensing fees, are the sole responsibility of the winners. Any litigation within the province of Quebec respecting the conduct and awarding of a prize may be submitted to the Régie des loteries et courses du Québec. All prizes will be awarded; winners will be notified by mail. No substitution of prizes is permitted.

4. Potential winners must sign and return any required Affidavit of Eligibility/Release of Liability within 30 days of notification. In the event of noncompliance within this time period, the prize may be awarded to an alternate winner. Any prize or prize notification returned as undeliverable may result in the awarding of that prize to an alternate winner. By acceptance of their prize, winners consent to use of their names, photographs or their likenesses for purposes of advertising, trade and promotion on behalf of Torstar Corp. without further compensation. Canadian winners must correctly answer a time-limited arithmetical question in order to be awarded a prize.

5. For a list of winners (available after 3/31/92), send a separate stamped, self-addressed envelope to: Harlequin Fashion A Whole New You Sweepstakes, P.O. Box 4694, Blair, NE 68009.

PREMIUM OFFER TERMS

To receive your gift, complete the Offer Certificate according to directions. Be certain to enclose the required number of "Fashion A Whole New You" proofs of product purchase (which are found on the last page of every specially marked "Fashion A Whole New You" Harlequin or Silhouette romance novel). Requests must be received no later than December 31, 1991. Limit: four (4) gifts per name, family, group, organization or address. Items depicted are for illustrative purposes only and may not be exactly as shown. Please allow 6 to 8 weeks for receipt of order. Offer good while quantities of gifts last. In the event an ordered gift is no longer available, you will receive a free, previously unpublished Harlequin or Silhouette book for every proof of purchase you have submitted with your request, plus a refund of the postage and handling charge you have included. Offer good in the U.S. and Canada only.

HQFW-SWPR

HARLEQUIN® OFFICIAL SWEEPSTAKES ENTRY FORM

4-FWHTS-2

Complete and return this Entry Form immediately – the more entries you submit, the better your chances of winning!

- Entries must be received by **December 31, 1991.**
- A Random draw will take place on **January 30, 1992.**
- No purchase necessary.

Yes, I want to win a FASHION A WHOLE NEW YOU Classic and Romantic prize from Harlequin:

Name _____ Telephone _____ Age _____

Address _____

City _____ State _____ Zip _____

Return Entries to: **Harlequin FASHION A WHOLE NEW YOU,**
P.O. Box 9056, Buffalo, NY 14269-9056   © 1991 Harlequin Enterprises Limited

PREMIUM OFFER

To receive your free gift, send us the required number of proofs-of-purchase from any specially marked FASHION A WHOLE NEW YOU Harlequin or Silhouette Book with the Offer Certificate properly completed, plus a check or money order (do not send cash) to cover postage and handling payable to Harlequin FASHION A WHOLE NEW YOU Offer. We will send you the specified gift.

OFFER CERTIFICATE

Item	A. ROMANTIC COLLECTOR'S DOLL (Suggested Retail Price $60.00)	B. CLASSIC PICTURE FRAME (Suggested Retail Price $25.00)
# of proofs-of-purchase	18	12
Postage and Handling	$3.50	$2.95
Check one	☐	☐

Name _____

Address _____

City _____ State _____ Zip _____

Mail this certificate, designated number of proofs-of-purchase and check or money order for postage and handling to: **Harlequin FASHION A WHOLE NEW YOU Gift Offer,** P.O. Box 9057, Buffalo, NY 14269-9057. Requests must be received by December 31, 1991.

ONE PROOF-OF-PURCHASE

4-FWHTP-2

To collect your fabulous free gift you must include the necessary number of proofs-of-purchase with a properly completed Offer Certificate.

© 1991 Harlequin Enterprises Limited

See previous page for details.